"Brilliant," Ryan said, leaning in to take the binoculars from Sasha. And that was his undoing. She was so close, he could feel her warmth, smell the roses.... He kissed her.

The jolt that went through him almost made him drop the binoculars. For an instant she stiffened, in shock he guessed, but then her mouth went soft, yielding. Heat singed along his nerves as the question he'd been carrying for so long was answered in fiery letters a foot high.

Yes. Yes, Sasha Tereschenko still sizzled his blood. She always had.

"Oh," she said when he finally broke the kiss, his pulse hammering. "That's...interesting to know."

He raised his brows in inquiry; actual words seemed beyond him at the moment.

"That it's still there."

"Oh, yeah," he managed. "It's still there."

Dear Reader,

Timing.

That's a thing that's always fascinated me. My brother-in-law once missed a flight from his workplace by mere moments. It went down, killing all aboard, minutes later.

Timing. How many things in life turn on timing? How many things might you have missed out on, how many things might you have escaped, all by the simple matter of timing?

Which got me to thinking about how often people meet someone they like, but for various reasons the timing is all wrong and it goes nowhere. But sometimes, people get a second chance. And if they're lucky, this time the timing is right, they are who they're supposed to be when they're supposed to be, and their lives change forever.

And that was the genesis of this book. It was Ryan and Sasha's time, and I hope you enjoy their story.

Happy reading,

Justine Davis

JUSTINE DAVIS

His Personal Mission

Silhouette®
Romantic
SUSPENSE

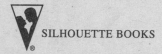

SILHOUETTE BOOKS

Recycling programs
for this product may
not exist in your area.

ISBN-13: 978-0-373-27643-1

HIS PERSONAL MISSION

Books by Justine Davis

Silhouette Romantic Suspense

Hunter's Way #371
Loose Ends #391
Stevie's Chase #402
Suspicion's Gate #423
Cool Under Fire #444
Race Against Time #474
To Hold an Eagle #497
Target of Opportunity #506
One Last Chance #517
Wicked Secrets #555
Left at the Altar #596
Out of the Dark #638
The Morning Side of Dawn #674
†*Lover Under Cover* #698
†*Leader of the Pack* #728
†*A Man To Trust* #805
†*Gage Butler's Reckoning* #841
†*Badge of Honor* #871

†*Clay Yeager's Redemption* #926
The Return of Luke McGuire #1036
**Just Another Day in Paradise* #1141
The Prince's Wedding #1190
**One of These Nights* #1201
*In His Sights #1318
**Second-Chance Hero* #1351
*Dark Reunion #1452
**Deadly Temptation* #1493
**Her Best Friend's Husband* #1525
Backstreet Hero #1539
Baby's Watch #1544
**His Personal Mistress* #1573

†Trinity Street West
*Redstone, Incorporated

Silhouette Desire

Angel for Hire #680
Upon the Storm #712
Found Father #772
Private Reasons #833
Errant Angel #924
A Whole Lot of Love #1281
**Midnight Seduction* #1557

Silhouette Books

Summer Sizzlers 1994
"The Raider"

Fortune's Children
 The Wrangler's Bride

JUSTINE DAVIS

lives on Puget Sound in Washington. Her interests outside of writing are sailing, doing needlework, horseback riding and driving her restored 1967 Corvette roadster—top down, of course.

Justine says that years ago, during her career in law enforcement, a young man she worked with encouraged her to try for a promotion to a position that was at the time occupied only by men. "I succeeded, became wrapped up in my new job, and that man moved away, never, I thought, to be heard from again. Ten years later he appeared out of the woods of Washington state, saying he'd never forgotten me and would I please marry him. With that history, how could I write anything but romance?"

Chapter 1

He had to do it, Ryan Barton told himself. What was a little personal humiliation, under the circumstances? He had no right to even worry about the odious task before him. He needed help, and the last person on earth he wanted to ask for it was the only one who could provide it. He couldn't stand even one more day of his parents' frantic worry.

Or his own.

He didn't like the word *frantic*. It contained an element of hysteria, and that was not a word he liked applied to himself. But he had to admit the more time that passed the more it fit; he'd gone beyond anxiety and worry a couple of days ago.

Trish, he thought, an image flashing through his mind of the blonde, blue-eyed little pest who had annoyed him endlessly in his early teenage years, even as he'd admitted to himself that he was flattered by her unwavering adoration of her big brother. And when he'd gotten himself in big trouble for hacking a corporate network, and been facing some serious consequences,

Trish had been the one who had defended him to their furious parents. That he'd known perfectly well he'd been in the wrong made her loyalty even more amazing to him.

And it had also been Trish who'd talked him into taking the unexpected offer made to him by the very person he'd been caught attacking. When Josh Redstone had challenged him to make the network he'd hacked safe from others with the same bent, it had been the beginning of his relationship with the vast Redstone empire. And now, seven years later, he couldn't imagine life without that connection. At Redstone he got everything that had been missing: the challenge, the equipment he never could have afforded on his own and the appreciation for his…less traditional skills.

That Josh Redstone had been the same age Ryan had been at the time when he'd begun that odyssey was one of the factors that had decided him. That, and that the alternative would likely have been a too-close acquaintance with bars and a cell somewhere.

He could, he knew, go to Josh with this. Anyone at Redstone could go to Josh with anything. And if Josh found out his little sister was missing, he would swing into action. But he also knew it was likely Josh would call in the Westin Foundation.

And that meant Sasha.

Ryan had met the dark-haired, dark-eyed Sasha a couple of years ago when Reeve had called for some tech help on the case of Josh's missing nephew. She had enthralled him with her bold beauty, her vibrant energy and spirit, and fascinated him with her exotic history.

It had taken him a long time to work up the nerve to ask her out. And no one had been more stunned than he when she'd said yes. But then, somehow, he'd managed to ruin things practically before they even began, and she'd walked away leaving him feeling like a spurned puppy.

And with the nagging feeling that that was exactly how she saw him, like an immature, bothersome puppy.

And now he had to ask her for help.

Only for you, Trish, he muttered to himself.

He dug his smart phone out of the pile of parts on his worktable; Ian's new, ultrasecure, wireless network router design was proving to be a bit of a challenge. But then, that was why he loved his job, and considered it a great honor to be working with Ian Gamble, Redstone's genius inventor.

At the last second he decided not to call Sasha directly. He still had her number in his phone—assuming it hadn't changed—but he didn't want her thinking this was just an excuse. This situation, and his concern for his little sister, was genuine, and calling the foundation would show her that.

So instead he found the number for the foundation and called it instead. As the call went through, he decided maybe the best approach would be to just pretend he'd forgotten all about their aborted relationship. Like it had meant nothing, that he'd thought about it no more than she likely had.

Yeah, that was it. That was the way to go. *Sasha Tereschenko? Yeah, I remember her. Works for the Westin Foundation, right? Met her a couple of times, I think....*

Sure, that would work. Never let her see you sweat, wasn't that how it went? So he wouldn't. Besides, he didn't, not really. It wasn't like he obsessed about it, about what had gone wrong. He'd moved on, just as she had. He hadn't been ready for any kind of permanence anyway.

No strings, that's the way for me, he'd said to himself, and two years later that hadn't changed. Not at all.

He really did barely think about it.

Which didn't explain why his stomach took a wild tumble when that unmistakable smoky voice rang in his ear.

"Westin Foundation, this is Sasha. How can I help?"

What the hell was she doing answering the phone? They had somebody who did that. Why was she—

He reined himself in, grimacing at his flustered reaction. It was like Sasha to just jump in if someone else was busy. She had no compulsions about job descriptions, only the job itself; he'd learned that about her early on. And he had a real, solid reason for calling, he reminded himself. *Get to it.*

"Do you have someone missing? I'm here, just tell me what you need."

What you need... That gentle, soft urging note had come into her voice, the tone that Ryan remembered so well. She could get a guy to eat broken glass with that voice, he'd thought then.

It hadn't changed.

"Yes," he said suddenly, not exactly sure what he was saying yes to. With an effort he shook off the effects of that voice. Thought about addressing her as Ms. Tereschenko, but that sounded so weird even in his head he abandoned the idea as soon as it formed.

"Sasha, it's Ryan. Ryan Barton."

"Ryan?"

Well, at least she only sounded surprised, and not like she had no idea who he was. That was something, he supposed, that she hadn't forgotten him completely.

"It's been a while. How are you?" She sounded, he thought, annoyingly cheerful.

"Okay," he answered, not quite able to sound the same.

"I heard about you helping with Gabe Taggert's missing wife. That was a good thing you did."

He was warmed by the words, but didn't like the fact. He didn't want to care at all. So he said, "I didn't do it. Ian's new metal detector did."

"But you ran it," she said. "If you hadn't found that car, he might never have known what happened to her. And I heard there were a couple of other missing persons cases closed because of the other things you found. Definitely a good thing."

"Yeah, well," he muttered, not knowing what else to say when he was thinking, *If I'm so great, why did you walk away?*

"So what are you—" She stopped suddenly. Then, quickly, "Wait. You said yes when I asked if you had someone missing."

Thankful she'd made the change, he shifted into the real reason he'd called. "Yes. My sister. For a week."

"Ryan, no!"

She sounded genuinely appalled, and that enabled him to get going on the things he'd planned to say.

"Yes. I know the foundation deals with children mostly, and Trish is eighteen, but only by five days. So the principles of searching can't be much different, can they?"

"It's very different looking for a teenager than a child," she said.

"I get that. Look, if you can't help, at least tell me how to start."

"Ryan, I never said that."

Her voice had taken on that gentle, coaxing tone again. Only this time it stung, made him think she'd put him into the category of frantic-relative-to-be-calmed. That that's exactly what he was didn't help any.

"Let's meet. Russ and I are just finishing up the paperwork on a case, but it should only take another half hour or so, then I'll be free."

Great, Ryan muttered to himself. Russell C. Langer, resident stud, *GQ*-handsome and so smooth he made Teflon seem like sandpaper.

And so hot for Sasha it was infuriating.

Or had been. He had no right to be infuriated anymore. And maybe Russ wasn't hot for her anymore.

Maybe he'd gotten what he wanted.

That thought made Ryan's stomach knot. Sasha's lively vividness and the polished, slightly older Langer's practiced charm made for…well, the perfect couple. Especially when contrasted with his own laid-back geekiness. Russ was all that, and he was none of it. At best, his sister's sometimes irritating friends called him cute, which was something he associated with little kids and puppies again, and thus not particularly flattering. Trish just told him he should be glad he didn't look like a typical geek, but he hadn't found much comfort in that.

"Shall I come there, or can you come here?" Sasha was asking.

There? At the foundation, where she and Russ were cozily working together? *No way,* he thought. *I so do not want to go there.*

Ryan shook his head sharply.

Trish, he ordered himself. *Get back to Trish, she's what really matters here, not your stupidity.*

"Ryan?"

"I… Let's meet in between."

"Okay." She didn't seem to find anything odd in the request. "It's lunchtime, how about at The Grill in an hour?"

"Great."

He wasn't at all hungry, but at least at the popular restaurant—known to locals as The Grill despite it's longer name involving the street it was on and the ethnicity of the owner—he could have some coffee, or a soda, something to do instead of staring at her like that pesky pup.

It would make it easier to hide the truth, that he'd never, ever forgotten her.

Ryan Barton, Sasha thought as she leaned back in her chair. She certainly hadn't ever expected to hear from him again. She'd known that he'd been bewildered by her sudden withdrawal, although she'd tried to explain. It wasn't that she hadn't liked him, she had. A great deal. It wasn't that she didn't have fun with him, she did. A great deal.

It wasn't that she wasn't attracted to him, she was. An even greater deal. Almost too much; she'd been nearly ready for a move to the next level, a sexual relationship, far too quickly for her comfort. There had been something about him that had, unexpectedly, appealed mightily to her. It wasn't his short, almost spiky hair that was nearly blond at the tips; that was hardly her style. More likely it was his obvious intelligence, his ready grin, his quick, energetic way of moving, and the simple fact that he'd made it clear he was strongly attracted to her.

But none of that changed the bottom line, the one difference between them that she simply couldn't get around. Ryan was cheerful, happy and carefree. The first two she liked. The last…well, it annoyed her. Ryan didn't worry about much of anything, even things that should be worried about. He seemed to have a blind faith that everything would work out the way it should.

And Sasha Tereschenko knew better.

But he'd called with something that seemed to have finally gotten through to him, she reminded herself. For the first time since she'd known him, Ryan had sounded…well, worried.

Maybe he would finally learn that life wasn't always a light-hearted skateboard through the park.

Quickly, she turned back to the paperwork she'd been working on when he'd called. If she pushed, she'd just make the time frame she'd given Ryan. She finished entering the text section of her report, then tackled the checklist at the bottom that would enter the case into their ever-growing database of cases, details and MOs in the case of criminal connections and the thankfully rare kidnappings.

When she was finally done, she attached the routing command that would complete the process. The computer software linked up with databases across the country, both law enforcement and private, and gave them an incredibly vast and broad-based pool of knowledge, statistics and case information to draw on. It was, to her knowledge, unique in the field, although thanks to Redstone, which had funded its development, it was being put into use all over the country.

And it had been written by Ryan Barton.

And there she was, back to the big conundrum. Shouldn't he get credit for that? Shouldn't the fact that he was making it easier for places like the Westin Foundation to find missing and endangered children count as evidence he wasn't utterly carefree?

She'd thought so. In fact it was one of the reasons she'd agreed to go out with him in the first place. But she'd learned early on it had been the challenge of making it work, not the desire to help, that had truly driven him. That was Ryan; he thought his blessed computers could do anything, if you just programmed them right. That his work often helped people was just a side effect.

Not that that didn't please him, but his focus was the machines, not the people. And that—

"Hey, beautiful, how about lunch to celebrate?"

Startled out of her reverie, she glanced up at Russ Langer, who was leaning against the doorjamb of her office. Funny, she thought. In the same way Ryan seemed to project his carefree mind-set, Russ projected self-assurance. She made herself use the term, even to herself, when what she was really thinking was cockiness. But she had to work with the guy, and thinking all the time he was a cocky jerk could lead to her actually saying it out loud, and she didn't want that.

Besides, he wasn't really a jerk, he was nice enough. And when he worked, he was good at it. It was simply that he was handsome beyond belief—and he knew it. She guessed he always had. She wondered yet again what it must be like to be able to slide through life simply on your looks.

"Well?" Russ prompted when she didn't leap to say yes to his offer.

"Sorry," she said, standing up and grabbing her phone to stuff it back in the capacious bag she called a purse. "A call just came in. I have to meet a…relative."

"We just finished a long one. Somebody else can go. We deserve a break."

"The family of a missing girl deserves a break," Sasha said pointedly.

Russ sighed. At least he'd learned that about her—nothing could distract her from helping someone who needed her particular talents.

"Want me to come with?" he asked as she reached the doorway, and him.

"No, I've got it. You go get your lunch, take your break."

His gaze narrowed over impossibly perfect cheekbones, as if he wondered if she'd meant the words as a slam. And perhaps, on some level, she had. She couldn't picture Russ ever skipping a meal or forgoing a break—even though he was right, it was deserved, the Novato case had been long and hard—to jump right into another case.

But he had offered, she reminded herself, and smiled at him. "I'll call you if it turns into something and I need the help. Thanks."

Appearing mollified, he nodded and moved aside so she could pass. She caught a whiff of expensive men's cologne. At least Ryan only smelled of soap and shampoo, she thought, much preferring the simplicity. It made the times when they'd gone out to dinner, when he had put on something, seem more special somehow. And his entire approach less...practiced.

God, woman, you are being ridiculous, she told herself as she walked through the building, a converted Tudor-style home that had once been known as "the purple place" for its odd paint job. Thankfully it no longer looked like a misplaced San Francisco row house, and blended in nicely with the others like it in the neighborhood that had once been residential gone seedy but was now a successful business area. Again, mostly thanks to Redstone, who had bought it specifically for a headquarters for the foundation; when Josh took an interest, the business world listened.

She walked out to her little yellow coupe, parked in the small courtyard they'd turned into a parking lot to avoid destroying the lovely garden they'd reclaimed from the front of the building. And every step of the way, she continued her self-lecture.

Just because the guy called out of the blue doesn't mean anything's changed.

She hit the button on her key, and the brightly colored car chirped and unlocked itself obediently.

He's got a problem, that's all, something he knows you're good at. He's probably got a steady girl by now, anyway, one who isn't so picky.

She yanked open the driver's-side door and tossed her big bag on the seat.

You're acting like you've been missing him all this time.

She got into the car and jammed the key into the ignition with more gusto than was needed. She hurried to start the car and head out. She needed to focus on driving.

So she could stop thinking about the irritating fact that her last thought had been true.

Chapter 2

Ryan watched Sasha thread her way past crowded tables back to the booth he'd managed to snag because he'd once bussed tables here. She was still the most amazing woman he'd ever seen.

She'd laughed when he'd told her that once, saying she had a mirror, thank you, and knew she wasn't beautiful. Striking, she could manage, she'd said. With the sense of a guy who'd just been asked if something made a woman look fat, he'd stumblingly answered, "That's what I mean. No, I meant… You're not… I mean, you are, but…different." He remembered that drowning feeling as he gave up and muttered, "You make it hard to breathe."

To his amazement her laughter had turned to a genuine smile. And she'd told him that was the nicest compliment she'd gotten in a while.

Things hadn't changed, he thought as he watched eyes lift and heads turn as she went by, a spot of bright, mobile color in the sunny yellow sweater she wore. It was, he knew, her favorite color, usually paired with black, "for contrast" she'd told him. She had a huge bag in the same colors slung over her shoulder; the bag was different, but the size the same as he remembered.

She'd cut her hair; that was about the only real change. And the short, sleek bob, longer at the front and sides than in the back so it moved every time she did, suited her. He usually preferred long hair, but there was something about the bare nape of her neck....

And then she was there, and he belatedly stood up, remembering his mother telling him a gentleman always did when a lady arrived. He thought such things ridiculously old-fashioned, but Sasha had also once told him she was an old-fashioned kind of girl, so he figured it couldn't hurt.

She smiled at him.

Score one for Mom, he thought as Sasha slipped into the booth opposite him.

Suddenly he couldn't think of a thing to say. He'd rehearsed in his head what he'd tell her about Trish, but he'd somehow forgotten to work on anything else. Desperate, his gaze landed on the brightly colored bag.

"Still carrying your life around, I see," he said, then groaned inwardly at the lameness of it.

"You never know," she said, as she always had when he'd teased her before about seeming to need a ton of stuff with her at all times. "Besides, it's a special bag. It was made for me by a friend." He looked more closely as she went on. "It was knitted, then washed in really hot water to shrink it. It's called felting."

"Shrink it?" he said, eyeing the thing that seemed the size of a large briefcase skeptically.

"It's perfect," she said, her voice taking on an imperious tone he hoped was teasing. "It's solid, sturdy, but nice and soft to the touch."

She stroked a finger over it as if to demonstrate. It was a

simple motion, and he had no explanation for the sudden hike in his pulse rate. He studied the bag for a moment, more to give himself a moment to collect himself than out of real interest, but when he did, he noticed the intricacy of the pattern.

"It looks like the geometric screen saver Ian uses."

Sasha laughed. "Maybe that's where she got the idea."

"She?"

"Liana Kiley."

His head came up then. "Liana? Our Liana?"

Sasha grinned. "I love the way you Redstone people are. Yes, your Liana. I figured you'd know her, given she works in your neck of Redstone, as it were."

He did know Liana. She worked for Lilith Mercer, who was cleaning up a mess left by the former head of the R&D division, a task he'd been involved in periodically, including some time spent with the pretty redhead. She was relatively new to Redstone, but that she was a perfect fit had become clear very early. Ryan liked her. And not just because she liked computers and was pretty good with them; she was a genuinely nice person.

And apparently a friend of Sasha's, which he hadn't known.

"Your colors," he said, not sure what else to say; that she was friends with someone he saw almost every day bothered him somehow.

"Liana called it 'Fright of the Bumblebee,'" she said with a grin.

He couldn't deny it fit; the explosion of yellow and black did look a bit like a bumblebee gone berserk.

The waitress arrived with two large glasses and set them down, along with a couple of menus, then left to give them time to look. Sasha looked at the glass, then at Ryan.

"I took a chance you're still into Diet Coke," he said.

She smiled. "As long as it's not decaf. I mean, what's the point?"

He laughed, and the knot in his gut loosened a bit. "Order something. I'm buying." She lifted a brow at him. "I called you," he pointed out.

"Point taken," she said, picking up the menu. "And since they fund us as well, I know how Redstone pays."

"I'm not hurting."

She looked up from the menu. "Not about that, anyway."

For an instant he thought she meant hurting about her, and he winced inwardly. Then he realized she had to mean Trish, and he felt like a fool, and worse, an uncaring idiot, for even momentarily forgetting the matter at hand.

"Tell me about your sister," she said in that soft, encouraging tone that had always made him want to go out and climb a mountain or slay a dragon, and not in any virtual world, but the real thing.

She'd never met Trish during the short time they'd been together, but he knew he'd told her about his little sister, probably with that exasperated tone most older siblings used. Although with ten years between them, he'd moved out on his own when she was nine, so he hadn't had to deal with the teenage angst on a daily basis.

And then he'd hacked himself into that colossal mess and she'd become a staunchly furious eleven-year-old defender, changing his view of his pesky little sister.

"She was there for me when I was in trouble," he said, only vaguely aware, lost in the memory, "and now I'm afraid she's in trouble."

"So you're going to be there for her," Sasha said, and the approval in her tone warmed him. "Tell me what's happened. Was there trouble at home?"

"No," he said quickly. "Not the kind that would make her take off. My folks are great."

"You've always said so," Sasha said. "But sometimes siblings see things differently."

He shook his head. "Trish got along fine with them. No fights, no blowups. Just the usual teenage stuff. She thought they were overprotective, but so did I."

"Sometimes," Sasha said again, this time carefully, "parents are different with girls."

Ryan considered this for a moment. "My dad was, a little. Extraprotective. But Trish could get around him, too, in a way I never could."

"Girls and their daddies," Sasha said. "It's a fact of life."

"Yeah. I envied her sometimes, when I was still at home. There she was, seven years old, wheedling things out of him that I couldn't get at seventeen. But it was hard to stay mad at her when she…" He trailed off awkwardly.

"When she adored her big brother?"

A sheepish smile curved his mouth. "Yeah."

"That's the natural order of things, too," Sasha said.

There was a pause as the waitress took their order—she still went for his own favorite cheeseburger, which likely meant, given she hadn't changed at all, she still worked out like a tri-athlete—and then she continued.

"You said it's been a week."

He nodded.

"And she just turned eighteen?"

He nodded again. "On the ninth."

"Any reason to think she didn't just take off on some celebration of her newly gained adulthood?"

And there it was, Ryan thought. The same wall they'd run into with the police. "Concrete reason? Like something I could show you?" He sighed. "No. The opposite, in fact."

"Opposite?"

"She left a note." To her credit, Ryan thought, her expression didn't change. "Not a suicide note," Ryan said quickly, since that was the first thing the cops had asked.

"I assumed it wasn't, or you wouldn't be talking to me, the police would be investigating. Are they?"

"No."

She merely nodded. "Do you have it?"

"No. My folks do." He shifted in his seat. "They didn't know I was going to call you."

"Will it bother them?"

Not nearly as much as it bothered me, he thought.

"I don't think so. They just want somebody looking for Trish, and obviously the police won't unless we come up with some evidence something's wrong. I mean they took a report, but it was pretty clear it wasn't going to go far."

"They have some big limitations," Sasha said. "So what did the note say? Any clues?"

"Thank you," he said impulsively. At her questioning look he tried to explain. "For not…instantly writing this off. For not giving me that look the cops did, the minute I told them about the note."

Although she looked pleased, she waved his thanks off with a gesture and refused to bash the police. "They have different priorities, and too darn many rules. We don't. And we have access to Redstone's resources. That's why we're so successful. So what did the note say?"

"Just that she had to go somewhere, not to worry, and she'd call when she could. But she's supposed to start college in the fall, at U.C. Davis. She wants to be a vet."

"And did she? Call, I mean?"

"No. And she's not answering her cell."

"Didn't even call friends?"

"Her best friend is spending the summer in Australia. Graduation present. She said she didn't know anything, even laughed at the idea of Trish taking off on her own."

Sasha nodded thoughtfully.

"Boyfriend?"

"No. She never dated much. She was focused on school. She was seeing one guy a year or so ago, but they broke up. I don't know why."

"Nasty break?"

Ryan looked uncomfortable. "I don't know. I only barely knew about the guy."

"Would your parents know?"

"Probably. They keep a close watch—" He stopped, as if realizing that however close his parents had watched their daughter, it apparently hadn't been close enough.

"I'll talk to them about it," Sasha said. "And I'll want to see the note."

"There was nothing in it about where she was going, or how long she'd be gone, or even if she'd be back. Nothing," he repeated in obvious frustration.

"Did she have a car?"

"Yes, my dad's old one, but it's at home still."

"How about finances? Credit card?"

"She had a checking account, and savings, but that's it. My folks wouldn't let her have a credit card, afraid she'd do the kid thing and get in way over her head."

"She'll get a million credit card offers once she gets to college," Sasha pointed out, refraining from stating her opinion on that common practice.

"They knew that. They just flat out told her she couldn't have one while she was underage and they might be held responsible for her irresponsibility, and that if she got one once she left the house, they wouldn't help her with it." One corner of his mouth quirked upward. "I got the same lecture at the same age."

"Good for your folks."

"I knew you'd say that," Ryan said, but with a smile.

"She's never expressed a desire to take off when she was old enough, see the country or the world?" Sasha asked.

"Trish? Hardly. She didn't even like going on family vacations. She's never even talked about wanting to go anywhere. She was looking forward to going to school, but she was even a bit nervous about that, it being so far away. In her eyes, anyway," he amended, as if realizing that to many people, especially those connected to a worldwide entity like Redstone, a distance of less than five hundred miles was almost negligible.

"So she's a homebody?"

He shrugged. "She liked life here. Her friends, going to the beach. And she volunteered a lot at Safe Haven."

"Safe Haven?"

"It's an animal shelter, sort of."

"Sort of?"

"It's mainly for the pets of people who have to go to the hospital, or older people who have to go into a nursing home, to take care of them while the owners can't."

Sasha smiled widely. "That's a wonderful idea."

Ryan nodded; even he had had to admit his little sister had found a worthwhile cause. "It's the main reason Trish wanted to be a vet, to come back and work for Safe Haven one day. They take care of the animals until the owner can take them back, and when it's an option, they take them to visit their owners until then. That's one of the things Trish was doing as a volunteer."

"Good for her."

"She was helping with adoptions, too, when they knew the owners wouldn't be able to take their pet back. They always try to place them with people willing to make the effort to continue the visits."

Sasha blinked. "To their original people?" Ryan nodded. "That's beyond wonderful, that's beautiful. Whoever thought of that should be very proud."

"Actually, there's a Redstone connection. Emma McClaren runs it. She's married to Harlan McClaren. Also known as Mac McClaren."

Sasha blinked. "The treasure hunter?"

"The same." He wasn't surprised she knew the name; anybody even vaguely aware of world happenings had heard of the man who had such a knack for finding and salvaging fortunes both sunken and buried.

"Wow." Her brow furrowed. "But what's the Redstone connection?"

Ryan grinned. "Who do you think bankrolled Josh Redstone when he was starting out?"

Her eyes widened. "Really?"

"And now he's Josh's right-hand financial go-to guy. He's got as much of a knack with finances and investments as he does finding treasure. And he's available to anybody who's Redstone. He's why even our file clerks have a retirement plan that's the envy of the corporate world."

"I had no idea."

"Few people do. Neither he nor Josh brags much."

"You're quite the Redstone booster, aren't you?"

He bristled slightly. "Redstone doesn't need me to boost it. It speaks for itself."

"That wasn't criticism. I have the highest opinion of Redstone, and Josh. We wouldn't exist if not for them, and him, and if we didn't, I'd be trying to get a job there."

"Oh." He felt a bit foolish.

"I like that you want to defend it, though."

He shrugged, tracing a path through the condensation on his glass. "I don't know where I'd be if Josh hadn't…been who he was."

She knew his story, he'd told her himself when he'd realized he wanted to keep seeing her. He'd told her before she'd heard it from someone else, not wanting her to get some slanted version of his youthful exploits as a malicious hacker who'd tackled Redstone just because they were the biggest kid on the block.

"So how's your retirement looking?" she asked. Startled, he looked up. Saw the twinkle of humor in her dark eyes. Felt the smile start to curve his mouth before he even realized he was doing it.

"Great," he said. "Even my dad approves. Thinks I'm finally being responsible. I haven't had the heart to tell him I signed up half because I wanted the kick of Mac McClaren doing my investing for me."

She laughed at that, but then, rather more intently, asked, "And the other half?"

Of course she hadn't missed that. He hadn't forgotten how rarely she missed anything. The very trait that made her so good at what she did also made her sometimes uncomfortably observant to be around. Especially if you were prone to sliding easily along the surface of life.

"I'm trying," he said at last. "Somebody told me once I didn't worry enough."

Her dark, arched brows shot upward. He'd startled her with that, since she'd been the one who'd said it.

"I doubt they said exactly that," she said.

"Close enough."

To his amazement, she seemed flustered. He'd never been able to manage that before, and he wasn't sure if it was a good or bad sign that he'd done it now. Before he could decide, their food had arrived.

The cheeseburgers were as good as always, but he wasn't able to give his the attention it deserved. Not with Sasha sitting across the table from him. He was grateful when, between bites—he'd always liked the fact that she enjoyed food—she turned back to the reason they were here.

"So this is uncharacteristic of your sister?"

"Very. Like I said, she loved living here, and her friends, and what she did at Safe Haven."

"Have you talked to them? The shelter?"

"I talked to one of the other volunteers. She said Trish left Emma a note saying essentially the same thing."

"Did she have a work schedule there, or as a volunteer did she just drop in whenever?"

He frowned. "I'm not sure."

"We'll check that out, then. And the girlfriend. Anyone else you can think of?"

The French fry Ryan had just swallowed seemed to jam in his suddenly tight throat. He hadn't realized just how much he'd needed somebody to believe, somebody to take his word for the fact that something was wrong with the way his sister had just up and left everything she knew and loved.

"You'll help?" he said, almost wonderingly.

"Of course," Sasha said. "It's what I do."

And if he was wishing she meant that personally as well as a representative of the Westin Foundation helping someone from Redstone, that was his problem, Ryan told himself. It didn't matter what he wished, or that he wished it from Sasha Tereschenko.

What mattered was that they find Trish.

Safe.

Chapter 3

"Is this taking you away from something else?"

Sasha glanced at Ryan in the passenger seat before pulling out into traffic; they were taking her car out to Safe Haven because he was low on gas and it was a long drive. And, as she'd pointed out, she got paid mileage.

"Not at the moment. That case we just finished was the only thing right now."

"You and…Russ."

"Yes." She saw something flicker in his eyes; he'd never liked Russ. And she was female enough to be flattered when she'd realized why.

"Is he still…"

"Hitting on me? Tirelessly."

"Did you ever give in?"

"No. Not," she added, "that it's your business."

"I know that."

He said it so quietly she changed her tone. "He only wants me because I don't want him. He finds that…hard to believe."

"He would," Ryan muttered.

Sasha stifled a smile.

"Happy ending?" he asked.

It took her an instant to make the shift. "The case?"

"Yeah."

She had to turn her attention back to her driving as a chance to get out of The Grill driveway presented itself—not something to be bypassed even midday in this busy area. It also gave her a chance to process the thought that she was surprised he'd asked. The old Ryan, the two-years-ago Ryan, wouldn't have even thought of that.

That she doubted he would have even cared back then was one of the reasons she'd walked away.

"Yes," she said once they had merged safely into the number two lane. "We found him in time."

"Little one?"

Again she was surprised. "Yes. Eight years old. Noncustodial parent took him."

"That's kind of common, isn't it?"

Now she was really surprised. "Yes. Yes, it is."

"I'm lucky my folks stayed together. Seems like all my friends' parents divorced, remarried, had more kids, divorced, and on and on."

"Yes, you are lucky," she said.

And she was stunned. His taking for granted the life he had had always irritated her. Was this appreciation sincere, or some effort to convince her he'd changed?

Get over yourself, she muttered inwardly. *It's not all about you, girl.*

"I appreciate your taking the time to help me. And even being willing to, when the police wouldn't."

There was undeniable sincerity in the words, and again she wondered at the formerly uncharacteristic attitude.

"They have their criteria, we have ours," she said. "Ours is relieving pain and worry."

"I know. I've always...admired what you do."

He'd told her that before, but in the aftermath of discovering how…well, face it, shallow he'd been at the time, she'd discounted that along with almost everything else he'd said as just surface chat to try to charm her.

Perhaps she'd been a little harsh before.

But right now there was something else she had to make clear. "You know that we can't force your sister to come back if she doesn't want to, now that she's eighteen."

"I know that."

"But we can find her and make sure she's all right."

"That's all I want. My folks want her home, but…I remember what it was like at that age."

He spoke as if that age were many decades behind him instead of merely one. That, too, was new.

She glanced at him again. He was staring out the windshield, but she noticed he was digging his left thumbnail into the side of his index finger, a habit she'd noticed before, the only sign he'd ever shown of being concerned about anything. That it had usually been about a complex computer problem he was dealing with had been the part that irritated her.

"Don't you ever worry about people?" she'd asked him once in exasperation.

He'd only shrugged. "With computers there's always an answer. You just have to find it."

She hadn't appreciated the logic and, she admitted later, the wisdom in that at the time. It had seemed just another sign that much as she liked and was attracted to him, their attitudes about some critical things simply didn't mesh.

"I don't want you to get into trouble," he said now, snapping her back to the present, his concern adding another layer to her surprise. "I know your focus is on kids, and technically Trish isn't one."

"But she's connected, through you, to Redstone. That's all Zach will need to hear. He'd do anything for one of Josh's people. It's once Redstone, always Redstone, for him. And of course, his wife is pure Redstone."

Sasha smiled as she said it; she greatly admired Reeve Westin, and had when she'd still been Reeve Fox. She'd been a bit intimidated at first, what with the incredible reputation of the Redstone security team, but Reeve had been wonderful, and for her own reasons staunch in her support of what the Westin Foundation did.

And not just because she loved the man responsible for its founding; the foundation had arisen out of the tragic murder of the Redstone Aviation's administrator's six-year-old son. It was funded in large part by Redstone, and was now headed up by Zach Westin himself. Another layer had been added when Westin had married Reeve, the member of the stellar Redstone security team who had been assigned to his son's disappearance. The latest in the growing string of Redstone couples.

"How are they? Zach and Reeve, I mean."

"Nauseatingly happy," she said with a grin.

"Figures," he said wryly. "I swear, it's in the water at Redstone these days."

"So I hear. Don't drink any, who knows what might happen to you."

He went very quiet then, and she wondered what about her somewhat-lame joke—which, if she was honest, had probably been a bit of a jab at him—had shut him up. For a moment she was afraid he was going to bring up the past, and she didn't want to deal with that. She'd put him safely and thoroughly behind her, and that's where she wanted him to stay. She was sure he'd probably done the same. After all, they'd only dated a few months. It wasn't like they had some huge, involved history between them. They'd had some good times, yes. If she were being honest again, some of the best times she'd ever had.

But you didn't build the kind of life she wanted on just good times. Well, that and incredible chemistry, she thought. Yes, that had definitely been there.

But it still wasn't enough. Not for the long haul. Not to end up where her parents had, married thirty-five years and still mad for each other. Or for that matter, like Ryan's parents, married nearly as long and in the same condition.

But where she appreciated, adored and wanted to emulate her parents, Ryan was embarrassed by his. He took them for granted, more amused by them than anything, and by their staying together through thick and thin when their contemporaries seemed to split like a stream around a rock anytime the slightest difficulty came up.

And then there was his embarrassment when they would engage in displays of affection in public, groaning that he preferred PDAs to be of the computer variety. Sasha had found them incredibly sweet, people to be admired, not embarrassed by. And Ryan had seemed bewildered when she'd pointed that out to him.

"How are your folks?" she asked now. "This must be awful on them."

"They're pulling together, as always." There was, Sasha noted, none of the usual embarrassment in his voice now.

"My mom keeps thinking it must be something she's done, my dad keeps telling her she's the perfect mother and it has nothing to do with her."

"Chances are he's right, it has nothing to do with her, or them. In a stable family like yours, it's often simply…being a teenager. Thinking you know everything. Rebellion against the status quo, all that."

It wasn't lost on her that these were some of the reasons Ryan had gotten himself into trouble all those years ago. He'd never denied to her that he'd started down the path that had led him into big trouble early on. He'd hacked his first system when he was sixteen, a simple one, that of his high school in an effort to improve his grades. It had been so easy he'd graduated quickly to other hacks.

He'd never gone for banks or financial institutions. Money wasn't his motivation. Once he'd taken on a gaming company, in an effort to get an advance look at a new game they were developing. Their security had been much tighter than the school's, and it had taken him a long time.

Redstone he had tackled when he was twenty-one, simply

for the challenge. He'd read an article on the brand-new Redstone genius Ian Gamble, who had developed a state-of-the-art firewall that had the computer security industry buzzing. It had taken him nearly a year to find a way past Gamble's ingenious design.

And if Ian hadn't been willing to take him on at Josh's request, Ryan didn't know where he'd be.

"They don't have any idea where she might have gone?"

"They've thought and thought about it, and can't come up with anything." He seemed to hesitate, then said quietly, "I'm worried about them."

"They'll probably be fine once we find her."

"I appreciate the confidence," he said. "And I know if anybody can find her, you can. But they seem full of…self-doubt. And part of that's my fault."

"Why?" she asked, startled at the sudden turn.

"First I go get into trouble, and now Trish essentially runs away from home? They thought they were doing a good job with us, but now they're questioning everything they've ever done."

Sasha had only met his parents twice, once by accident when they'd dropped by Ryan's apartment when she was there, and once after the breakup, when she'd gone by Redstone to return a CD he'd lent her and they'd been visiting. She'd liked them both times. Enough to wish things had gone differently. They seemed to her the epitome of the backbone of America, the kind of people who really made things work, the kind she admired and respected.

She didn't like the thought of them second-guessing their entire lives.

"I'll talk to them. Maybe I can help them see that's not true."

He seemed relieved at that idea. So he did care, she thought.

"Will they be home tonight?"

He nodded. "Dad gets home about six, and mom's always home in the afternoons."

"Is she still working for that doctor?"

"Yeah. And Dad's still crunching numbers at the bank."

She remembered suddenly how he'd once told her his dad had to be the most boring guy on the planet. Same boring work, at the same boring place, for over twenty years. That had been, she realized in retrospect, the beginning of the end. The dismissive assessment had angered her. She couldn't be with someone who didn't realize the value of that, who didn't make the connection between that kind of steadiness and his own comfortable, carefree life.

And she'd told him so, in no uncertain terms.

"Almost as boring as sitting at a computer all day," she said, not bothering to keep the snap out of her voice. And then wondering why; it wasn't like it mattered anymore.

"Computers aren't boring!" His defensiveness was quick, instinctive. "They've changed the world, made amazing things possible." He gestured at the GPS screen set into the dash of her car. "You'd be fumbling with maps if you didn't have that thing to give you turn-by-turns right to Safe Haven's front door."

"True enough," she had to admit.

"They're not boring at all."

As they pulled to a stop at a red light, she turned slightly to look at him.

"Did you ever think that maybe numbers aren't boring to your father? That maybe he likes the…the logic of them, the symmetry, the balance? Did you ever think that your blessed computers are based on numbers, and that you probably inherited some of your father's knack with them, and that that's the reason you're good with them?"

She could see by his expression that he hadn't.

The light changed. As she turned her attention back to driving, she was inwardly chiding herself for coming down so hard. This was, after all, none of her business anymore. It probably never had been. But it had been a measure of how much she liked the guy that she'd even tried to change his attitude about some things that were very basic to her.

Teach you to be a foolish female, try to change a male who doesn't want to change, she thought, and not for the first time.

"Sorry," she said into the silence of the car, "you came to me for help, not criticism."

She heard him let out a compressed breath before he said levelly, "If one's the price for the other, I'll take it."

Now that was a change, she thought, surprised anew.

"Besides," he went on, "I realize now how you could spend twenty years in the same place. I never want to leave Redstone. I still don't get the accounting thing, but what you said about the numbers…that makes sense."

My God, Sasha thought. *He really has changed.*

The old Ryan would have either laughed her off, or gotten even more defensive.

Had he finally grown up? Had the boy who had wanted only to slide along smoothly, the only challenges he enjoyed coming from his beloved computers, finally realized that people were what really mattered?

She didn't know. Couldn't be sure, at least, not yet. Maybe he was just putting on a front of connecting with real people, knowing—because she'd told him so bluntly—that she thought him lacking that skill.

And there you go again, making it all about you. When did you get so stuck on yourself?

She lectured herself for another moment, ending with the truth that there was only one thing she could be sure of at the moment: that her own, deep-down reaction to the possibility was unsettling. She shouldn't care, it shouldn't matter, she'd left Ryan Barton long behind.

Hadn't she?

Chapter 4

Sasha was still pondering the changes in Ryan, wondering just how deep they went, when the GPS he'd been so enamored of announced their destination was one mile ahead on the right. She slowed, looking, and saw a long, low, red-barn-style building set back from the road. A smaller one was off to one side, and what had apparently once been a small house sat at the end of a long driveway behind a secured gate.

The traditional rail fencing was high, and screened on the inside to make it secure, but painted pristinely white so that the first thing you thought of was charm rather than serious function. The grounds were tidy and well kept, and the small pack of five dogs who raced along the fence to greet them, tails up and tongues lolling, gave a homey air to it all.

"They look happy," Sasha said as she pushed the button on the gate beneath the small plaque with those instructions.

"Yeah. And healthy."

The little house was clearly the office, and was surrounded

with plants, trees and flowers that looked as happy and healthy as the dogs. Beside the house Sasha saw a path that led through a big, open field toward a thick grove of trees, where it disappeared invitingly into the deep shade.

They went up two steps to the broad front porch, and stopped at the bright red front door.

"This is quite a place," she said as she looked around.

"We like it," came a female voice from inside the door where they'd stopped. "Come on in."

The interior of the office was as tidy as the grounds. Sasha couldn't help smiling at the photos on the walls, images of animals captioned imaginatively in the vein of a popular Web site that she'd come across recently, the funny spelling contributing to the humor.

"Very nice place," Sasha said. "I'm Sasha Tereschenko," she added, offering her hand to the young woman coming toward them.

"I'm Sheila McKay," the woman said, drying her hands on a bright blue towel before she held out a hand first to Sasha, then Ryan. "I sort of run this place, when the real boss is away."

"Mrs. McClaren?"

Sheila blinked at Ryan. "Yes. You know her?"

"Of her. I work for Redstone."

The smile that lit the woman's face made Sasha reassess her looks; she'd thought her a bit plain at first, although her shoulder-length hair had a lovely reddish tint that went well with her fair skin and the faint sprinkling of freckles across a pert nose. But that smile could light up a city block, Sasha thought now.

"Bless Redstone," Sheila said fervently. "We were nearly going under, a few years back. The rent kept going up, the county was threatening to rezone us, we could barely keep up with the maintenance."

Sasha looked around. "Obviously that's not a problem now. This place is perfect."

"Well, not quite. But we own the land now—it was Emma's wedding present from her husband—and Emma's got big plans. An aviary, so the birds we get have room to fly, if they can. And her husband's building a corral for us out back, because Emma wants to take on a couple of abused horses the county shelter doesn't have room for."

"He's building it? Himself?" Sasha asked, startled at the idea of a man like Mac McClaren doing something so mundane.

"Yep. For a rich guy, he's pretty handy," Sheila said with a grin. "And we love him around here. He's made it all possible. Anything Emma wants for this place, she gets. Including the county off our back, since they surely don't want to make Redstone mad. Or have Mac McClaren, famous treasure hunter, talking to the press about their interference in our innocent, benevolent enterprise."

"Wise," Ryan said with a crooked grin back at her.

"Yes. Now, what brings you here? Do you need us to take an animal?"

"No," Sasha said, "it's something else."

"Then how can I help you?"

"It's my sister," Ryan said.

Sheila looked puzzled. "Your sister?"

"Trish Barton."

Sheila looked startled. "You're Ryan?"

He nodded. Sheila looked him up and down, then smiled impishly. "Well, she was right. You are cute."

Sasha smothered a grin as Ryan flushed. She knew that term grated on him. It always had. She sort of understood, *cute* was such a high school term. But he was cute, there was no getting around that. And she had the feeling that with his boyish face, he'd still be cute at fifty.

"Better than pretty," she said to the room at large, and Sheila's laugh got them through the moment, even though it made Ryan grimace.

"I don't think we realized how hard Trish worked around here until now," Sheila said. "I know I didn't. I'm trying to pick up the slack, but the therapy program alone has me exhausted."

"Therapy?" Sasha asked. "For the animals?"

"No," Sheila said. "We started a program where we take animals to visit nursing homes and hospitals, to cheer up patients. Started with one dog, a very special one, and Whisper did so well we've now got three dogs, a cat, two hamsters and a ferret in the program."

"A ferret?" Ryan said, distracted.

"Kids," Sheila explained with a smile. "They love the dogs, but they're fascinated with the more unusual stuff."

"And…my sister did this?"

Sheila frowned. "Yes. You didn't know?"

"I know she took the animals to visit their owners a lot, but not about this part."

"You should be proud of her. She has built up that program almost by herself, from the moment Emma gave her a shot at it. She has more energy than the rest of us put together."

"She is…happy here?" Sasha asked carefully.

Sheila looked puzzled. "Very. Emma always has to be careful to make sure she doesn't neglect the rest of her life to do it, always nagging her about schoolwork, and telling her she should have a social life, too."

She shoved a hand through her hair, brushing back a lock that stubbornly wanted to fall over her forehead. It looked like she was growing out bangs, Sasha thought, an annoyance she'd been through herself a time or two before she'd settled on the sleek bob she wore now.

"We were glad she finally took that advice. How's her trip going? Will she be back soon?"

Sasha saw Ryan's reaction, the disappointment in his eyes that this woman apparently didn't know any more than he did.

"You haven't heard from her?" Sasha asked.

"Since she left? No. We're all hoping she's having too much fun."

"What did she tell you about where she was going?"

Sheila glanced at Ryan, obviously assuming he must already know all this; after all, Trish was his sister.

You don't know Ryan, Sasha thought. *He likes his world without ripples.*

And even as she thought it, she realized that for all the difference in his talk, it seemed Ryan hadn't really changed at all. Not at heart.

And that, she thought sadly, was where it mattered the most.

"Just that it was somewhere she'd never been. And that she'd heard it was beautiful there."

"Where?" Ryan asked, as if he couldn't hold back any longer.

"She didn't say," Sheila answered. Then, curiously, "Don't you know?"

"No one does," Ryan said flatly.

Sheila's eyes widened. "Not even your folks? That doesn't sound like Trish."

"Exactly," Ryan said.

"She hasn't called them, either? Or you?"

"No. Or answered our calls. And her voice mail is full."

"That's very odd. She adores you."

Ryan flushed again, but his voice held a note of bitterness when he said, "So much she wouldn't even tell me about this."

Maybe she thought you wouldn't understand, Sasha thought, but kept that to herself as she asked, "She didn't say anything else, even in passing, about where she was going or why?"

Sheila seemed to hesitate for a second. "Not directly, no."

"Then indirectly?"

"Nothing she said. But…"

"But what?" Ryan said urgently.

Sheila studied him for a moment, and Sasha saw the moment when the woman realized what was really happening. "You're afraid for her," she said, worry suddenly transforming her face. "You think something's happened to her?"

"We don't even have a clue that anything's happened. But for Ryan's parents' sake, we want to be sure."

Sheila shifted her focus to Sasha. "Are you a friend of Trish's?" she asked, somewhat belatedly.

"More of Ryan's," Sasha said. "I have some…practice looking for people, so I'm helping out."

Sheila wasn't distracted by the purposeful vagueness. "Are you a cop?"

"No. I'm only here as a friend."

"Are you Redstone?"

"No," she said again. "Except by extension. Where I do work is funded in part by Redstone."

"Oh. Kind of like us, then."

"Yes, I imagine so."

Finally, the woman seemed content to leave it at that. Sasha was glad; sometimes just the idea of the Westin Foundation being called in frightened people. They'd handled several high-profile cases, and some of them had not ended prettily. The case the foundation had been born of, the kidnapping and murder of Zach Westin's small son, had been one of the ugliest.

"What was it you were thinking, Sheila? At this point, anything will help."

The woman's mouth twisted slightly, as if she weren't sure what she'd thought wasn't silly.

"Before she left Trish was acting…different. Excited. Almost giddy. We all thought it was graduating high school, turning eighteen, all that. But then she told us she was going on this trip, her first one ever by herself, and it seemed obvious that was what had her so wound up."

Sasha listened silently, and when Ryan opened his mouth as if to speak she hushed him with a gesture.

"And…?"

Sheila lowered her gaze. "It's just a feeling I got. Nothing I can say for sure."

"Sometimes feelings are more accurate than what we think we see," Sasha said.

"It was just the way she talked about it. Like there was more than just the trip she was looking forward to. She never said, but…I don't know. Maybe it's just that we don't remember how exciting that first solo trip can be."

"Did she talk about what she was taking? Shopping for things to take, that kind of thing?"

She sensed rather than saw Ryan grimace, as if he thought the question foolish. She didn't care; she knew what she was doing.

"You know, she did say something one day about having to find a heavier jacket. She said it was going to be hard to do in Southern California in the summer."

Sasha sensed Ryan's sudden alertness. *Not so foolish after all,* she silently told him.

"When did she first start talking about this trip, do you remember?"

"Shortly before she graduated," Sheila said. She flicked a glance at Ryan. "We thought maybe the trip was a graduation present, from her folks or something. That maybe that was why she wouldn't talk about any details, that it was supposed to be a surprise, and she didn't want to let on that she'd found out about it. But I guess that wasn't it, was it?"

"No," Ryan said grimly. "We didn't know anything about it."

Before Sheila could react to that, Sasha asked, "Do you still have the note she left here?"

"I don't know. She left it for Emma. She might have kept it. I can ask."

"Please do." She handed Sheila one of her Westin Foundation cards, figuring it didn't matter now if the woman knew where she worked. "My number's on there, if you could let me know as soon as possible."

She definitely wanted that note, she thought. She wanted to compare it to the one left at home. If they were different, that would be significant—people often told the people they worked with different things from what they told their family. Especially if those people shared the bond of dedication the people of Safe Haven seemed to.

If they were the same, that would also be significant, indicating Trish had been truly intent on keeping her secret. Or secrets.

If they were identical, that would be even more significant, Sasha thought grimly. There were few circumstances where a person used exactly the same wording, and not many of them were very good.

"You don't really think anything bad has happened, do you?" Sheila asked, anxiety breaking into her voice now, especially after she'd read the business card. "We all love Trish, she's so dedicated, and Dr. Burke thought she had a real chance to make it as a vet."

"Dr. Burke?"

"Elizabeth Burke. She's retired now, but she donates her services to us. Trish worked with her a lot, made a point to be here to assist anytime she was scheduled to visit. I think that's what inspired Trish to want to go to veterinary school."

"There's no reason yet to think anything bad has happened," Sasha reassured the woman.

They were walking back to Sasha's car when Ryan's cell phone rang. Once she was sure it wasn't the errant Trish, Sasha walked ahead a little, to give him some privacy.

She thought about what Sheila had told them. If Trish had been excited about more than just a trip alone—to, apparently, a cooler clime—Sasha was willing to bet she was right.

"My folks are home," Ryan said, catching up with her. "Dad can't concentrate at work. He's really worried."

"Then let's head there. I want to see the note, and talk to them, let them know that something's being done. That means a lot."

"Thank you," Ryan said.

There was no denying the fervency.

"You really do care about them."

His sandy brows lowered. "Of course I do. Just because I don't talk about it every waking minute doesn't mean I don't care. I love them, and I love my sister."

Sasha's brows shot upward in turn. She tried to remember if he'd ever been prodded to such a stinging retort when they'd been together. She didn't think so. When she had a moment, she'd ponder that change, along with the rest.

She drove, following the directions he'd programmed into the GPS—never mind that he'd never seen this exact system before, it seemed no computer was beyond his scope—wondering yet again if he'd actually grown up in the past two years.

And steadfastly not wondering why it seemed to matter so much.

Chapter 5

"The note she left at home, was it handwritten?"

Ryan snapped out of his thoughts, which had been focused mainly on how, if they'd been closer, Trish might have told him where she was going and why.

That had always been one of Sasha's main complaints about him; family was everything to her, and she couldn't understand his attitude toward his own. She'd more than once told him if anything ever happened to one of them, he'd be sorry he'd taken them for granted.

He'd blithely brushed it off as a skewed view because of the work she did. But now…

He made himself focus on her question. "No. It was printed, on her ink-jet printer. Why?"

"Hand-signed?"

"Yes. And she handwrote 'Don't worry,' at the bottom. As if," he ended with another grimace. "Why does it matter?"

"Not sure it does yet. Is that her normal way of communicating? Does she leave notes often?"

"I don't know if she does at home. She usually texts me."

"Does she use computers like you do?"

He gave her a sharp look. "What's that supposed to mean?"

"This isn't about you, Ryan," she said. "I'm just asking if this would be her typical way of doing this, leaving a computer-generated note rather than a handwritten one."

"Oh." At her patient tone, he felt like a fool. "Yes, she probably would. She uses her laptop for most things like that, but she's not…into them like I am."

"Few people are," Sasha said, and Ryan reined in his initial gut reaction with the ease of long practice. He'd heard the sentiment, often in tones of derision, too many times to get upset, he told himself.

That it still stung coming from her was something he'd just have to deal with.

"But to be fair," she went on, "few people can make them dance to order like you can, either."

He blinked. "I… Was that a compliment?"

She looked surprised as she glanced at him. "Of course it was. That software program you wrote for us, the one that links us to all the databases, that's been an incredible help."

"Oh." A kernel of warmth blossomed inside him.

"I could tell you about at least half of my past ten cases where something we found with your system got things going when we were at a loss. And at least three of those…well, it probably made the difference between life and death."

Startled, Ryan turned in his seat and stared at her. "You mean that literally?"

"I do," she said firmly.

"That's…wow."

She glanced at him. "That wasn't why you did it though, was it?"

He looked away, shifted his gaze to the front, through the windshield again, his thumbnail digging into the side of his finger.

"I admit," he said finally, "when they asked me about doing

it, it was just a challenge. Setting up all the parameters, the search engine, the query path, all of that, and to get it to work with all the different databases when each one was set up slightly differently."

"You were focused on the how, not the why."

"Yes," he said, glad she understood at least that much. They'd talked about this when they'd been together, but she hadn't listened to him before. She'd been so astonished that the why, helping find lost souls, hadn't been the moving force behind his work, that she'd been almost angry with him.

One of the many times she'd been almost angry with him.

And he hadn't understood. Not at all. "If the end result is what you need, do the reasons matter?" he'd asked.

"Only because I was starting to care about you," she'd retorted.

He'd realized later that was the beginning of the end.

"So it doesn't bother you now that my motivation wasn't the same as yours?" he asked, wondering if he was going to regret asking.

"No," she said. "Not now."

He smiled, relieved, although not quite sure why it still mattered after all this time.

It wasn't until they pulled up in front of the house he'd grown up in that it occurred to him that perhaps he shouldn't be relieved at her words at all. That "not now" merely meant it didn't bother her because she truly didn't care.

No surprise, Barton. You knew that.

No, no surprise that she didn't care.

The surprise was that it stung.

"Your home is lovely," Sasha said.

"Thank you," Joan Barton said.

Ryan watched his mother bustle around, fussing over the plate of cookies she'd put out with the fresh coffee she'd served. He knew it was just her way—when she was worried, she fussed—but Sasha didn't. He should have warned her.

Then again, maybe not; she seemed unflustered by it. Indeed, she'd been effusive in her thanks, and her compliments about the house, especially the colorful garden out front, his mother's ongoing pet project, the cookies, the coffee, everything.

Ryan thought she was going a bit over the top. It was just a house, after all, and the cookies were good, but his mom made them all the time, it wasn't anything unusual. But Sasha was chatting away, as if she were worried about making a favorable impression.

As if he'd brought a date home to meet the parents, he thought suddenly, tensely. The idea put a whole new light on her easy chatter.

"Your home is also very comfortable," Sasha was saying. "In my parents' place, you're almost afraid to move. My mother, she collects. Mostly small, breakable things."

"Dustcatchers," Joan said with a laugh. "That's what Patrick calls them."

Sasha looked at his father and smiled. "And right you are."

"Hate all that clutter," he muttered, but he smiled back at her.

Ryan realized abruptly that this was the first time in a week he'd seen a real smile out of either of his parents. And certainly the first time he'd heard his mother laugh, even though it had been a bit faint.

He looked at Sasha with a new admiration. He'd never seen her work before, but if this was how she did it, he was impressed. In a matter of minutes, she'd not only charmed them, but relieved at least some of their tension.

He felt a little silly. He should have known there was good reason that she'd become so quickly indispensable at the foundation.

"I remember you," Patrick Barton said suddenly. Then, with a sideways glance at his son, he added, "Always thought Ryan should never have let you get away."

"Dad!"

It burst from him before he could stop it. And he wished he had stopped it; he would have liked to hear what Sasha's answer to that would have been. But after his yelp, she merely smiled.

"I thank you for the compliment," Sasha said. "Now shall we get to why I'm here?"

"I thought your foundation only worked with children? The police keep telling us Trish isn't one anymore," Joan said, sounding aggrieved.

Sasha hesitated for a moment, and Ryan wondered if she'd guessed that his mother had asked not only out of curiosity, but to delay the inevitable. He also wondered how she'd answer.

"I'm not here officially, but as a friend," she finally said. "I work missing children cases mostly, but I thought perhaps I could help. The fact that there's no sign Trish is in danger doesn't mean you're not still worried."

Ryan could almost feel his mother relax slightly, and his admiration grew into awe at how easily and quickly Sasha accomplished what he'd been trying to do for a week.

"And," Sasha added, "I know it's hard to talk about it like this, because it's admitting she's gone and facing how frightening it is."

And just like that she put her finger on the reason his mother had been acting like this was merely a social occasion. Or trying to.

"It's horrible," his mother whispered.

Hearing the pure pain in her voice, Ryan ached to ease it, to do something, but he didn't know what. His mother was generally a cheerful, easygoing woman, always looking on the bright side. He supposed that was where he got his own usually sunny outlook.

And then his father moved, sitting next to her on the sofa, putting his arm around her. His mother leaned into him, taking a deep, shuddering breath. Then, as if she'd drawn strength from the gesture, she seemed to pull herself together, even sitting up straighter. That was all it took, a simple move by his father?

He realized then that, even had he tried, he couldn't have comforted his mother so well. In an odd, abrupt shift of perspective, Ryan suddenly saw them as if they weren't his parents. He saw them as a couple, a unit, still in love after thirty-two years. The size of that suddenly struck him, and it was a jolt. What must it feel like, that kind of permanence? He'd always thought of it as being tied to one person, limiting, confining.

But now he sat here in shock, thinking there were aspects he'd never considered before. Having one person who knew you, knew what you needed before you asked, who would go to any lengths to provide it, one person you could trust implicitly, who would ever and always have your back, one person who would always be there for you….

He snapped out of his reverie as Sasha switched into high gear. She asked for a copy of Trish's senior photo, which his mother quickly got. Then the note Trish had left, and permission to take it with her; one of the experts at the foundation, an ex-cop named Bedford, had a knack for reading between the lines, she said.

"I'm sure you've been wracking your brains," she said then, "trying to figure out if she said anything, mentioned anything you've forgotten."

Patrick nodded. "I can't believe she just did this, and we had no idea. I always thought we were a close family, but obviously we weren't paying enough attention," he ended bitterly.

Ryan didn't think anybody paid more attention—often too much for his own comfort—than his parents, but that didn't seem the right thing to say just now. He left it to Sasha to answer.

"That's not necessarily true. From what Ryan's told me, you had no reason to think she wouldn't want a typical, fun-filled summer here before she headed off to college."

"No," Joan said, a tremor creeping into her voice. "No reason."

"So let's deal with other things. What did she take with her, and what did she put it in?"

"Her big suitcase is gone. She must have planned to be gone for some time." The tremor strengthened. "What if she never comes back, what if we never know?"

"It's way, way too early to even think about that," Sasha said, then went on briskly. "This boy she dated for a while, have you spoken to him?"

"Troy? Yes. But they broke up when he transferred schools when his folks moved to San Diego. He hasn't heard from her."

"Have you looked through her closet? What clothes did she take?"

"Now that was odd," Joan said, taking her cue from Sasha's businesslike tone. "She left most of her summery things."

"So she took fall clothes? Or winter?"

Ryan had no idea what that meant; to him winter meant you put on a jacket. But obviously his mother understood, so it had to be a girl thing.

"Warmer things. She doesn't have true winter clothes, since she's lived here all her life."

"And we have no real winter," Sasha agreed with a smile. "So, what else? Anything obviously missing, or not so obvious?"

"Her laptop," Ryan put in. "She has a smart phone, but she took the laptop, too."

Sasha looked at him. "What does that indicate to you? I mean, I know for you that means you'll be gone for the afternoon, but for her?"

Ryan winced inwardly, but remembering her earlier words, didn't react to the teasing. Besides, his mother laughed, and that was worth a lot. And when Sasha glanced at Joan Barton and smiled, he realized that had been her intent all along.

"She used the phone for day to day, I think. I got more texts than e-mails."

Sasha nodded. Then she turned to his mother. "May I see her room?"

"Of course."

They went up the stairs, and Ryan started to walk down the hallway.

"Right here," his mother said, startling him as she stopped in front of the first door on the right.

"She moved into my room?" *How did I not know that?*

"A couple of years ago. She wanted the window seat," his father said. "And it's a little bigger."

The window seat. That triggered a memory, of Trish saying something about that. So, maybe he had known, and had just forgotten?

More likely filed it under "unimportant," you jerk, he told himself. *And now she's gone.*

"And," his mother said, putting a hand on Ryan's arm, "she wanted to be in her beloved big brother's old room."

"Aw, Mom," he muttered, in light of his own thought, much more comfortable with his father's prosaic explanation.

Maybe that's why they worked so well together, he thought. His father's reality-based practicality balanced his mother's rose-colored glasses outlook. The insight—something he suspected he should have realized long ago—again made him look at them in a new way.

And again he thought of the solidity of them as a team, together for over three decades, a united front, never alone in life…yeah, maybe there were advantages. He could even see himself wanting someone like that, that solid, unwavering, always-got-your-back kind of person.

What he couldn't see was ever being that kind of person for someone else.

Stepping inside what had once been his domain was strange, especially given how different it looked. Gone were his posters of video games—where had Lara Croft ended up?—and the shelves full of computer gear and software boxes. The corner where he'd had his CD player and music now held hers, a unit that turned her portable into a full-on sound system. He had helped his folks pick it out for her.

Trish had painted the room a soft green, and the trim around the windows bright white. It looked, he had to admit, pretty good. Maybe his black wall—his mother had only allowed him to paint one—had been a bit oppressive. On the walls were some things he recognized, prints of horses running free, and framed photos.

He stopped in front of one in particular, a shot from the last vacation they had all taken together, the year before he'd graduated from high school. His parents looking amazingly, as they did now, Trish, a lively-looking child with a tangle of sandy brown hair the same shade as his own, and himself, thin, gangly and awkwardly teenaged, zits and all.

They'd gone to Yosemite, and while he'd groused mightily about the boredom of it, complained that he'd wanted to stay home and hang with his friends, the memories from that trip were among the most vivid—and best—he had.

The sights, from the amazing two-tiered drop of Yosemite Falls to the towering, unbelievable and almost otherworldly mass of Half Dome, were a dose of genuine reality he'd never forgotten, images no amount of virtual reality could match.

He hadn't even minded the constant presence of then seven-year-old Trish tagging at his heels. He'd even been watchful of his little sister, out in the real world where big animals—the favorites of the already-set-on-her-life's-path Trish—roamed and smaller critters milked the millions of visitors for all the free food they could get.

If there hadn't been ten years between them, would they have stayed closer? Would he perhaps have seen some sign, some clue about what was to come? Would she maybe even have confided in him, the way she once had?

Or was it not the age difference, but his own fault, for being so wrapped up in his own life and world? Was Sasha right, had she been right two years ago? Was he truly that insular, that shallow?

He stared at the image of his little sister, at the way, in this photo, she looked up at him with what he couldn't deny was childlike adoration. Had he taken what he had so for granted that he'd lost it?

Where the hell are you, Trish? And why?

His mother's plaintive words echoed in his mind. *What if she never comes back, what if we never know?*

That wouldn't happen. It just wouldn't. He wouldn't let it. And Sasha wouldn't.

He knew that, on some deep gut level he didn't even question. If there was a way to bring Trish home, or at least to find her safe and explain all this, Sasha would do it. If there was one thing he'd always known about her it was that there was no way she would give up.

Ever.

Chapter 6

"Does Trish have a page or pages on any of the social networking sites?" Sasha asked.

"No," Patrick said.

"Yes," Ryan said.

Father and son both blinked as they looked at each other.

"I see," Sasha said.

"She does?" Joan asked her son.

"Well, yeah. She's a teenager. They all do, I think."

"When was the last time you looked?"

Ryan shifted uncomfortably. "Right after she set one up, about a year ago. She asked me to, asked for my opinion."

"But you didn't check it with any regularity?"

"Not once she got it going. Her friends there are mostly teenage girls who punctuate everything with OMG."

"OMG?" Joan asked.

"Oh, my God," Sasha explained, still looking at Ryan, who grimaced.

"Anyway, it gets old. And I guess I kind of forgot until you asked just now."

He sounded more than just sheepish, he sounded remorseful. Sasha couldn't imagine having a sibling and not wanting to know what they were doing, but perhaps that was because she had none.

"We'll check," Sasha said, then turned back to his parents. "Has Trish asked for more money than usual lately, or been gone more?"

"Well, more money for things to go away to school," Joan said. "We've gone shopping for things for her dorm room several times."

"But nothing for solo shopping trips?"

"Sometimes, if there was something specific she wanted."

"And did she always come back with that thing?"

Joan frowned. "Yes, why?"

Ryan was watching her steadily, understanding clear on his face; he, at least, knew she was trying to find out if Trish had been squirreling away money.

"She had a small trust fund, same as I did, from our grandfather," Ryan said. He glanced at his mother. "Was it the same for Trish, she couldn't touch it until she was eighteen?"

Joan nodded. "But she hasn't, I'm sure. She knows it was for college expenses."

"I'll check," Patrick said, and got up to make a phone call.

Joan was frowning, but answered the other part of Sasha's question. "As for being gone, it was the opposite. She was home more. I assumed it was because she wanted to be, since she was going to be off to Davis in a couple of months. Although she seemed to spend most of the time in her room, talking with her friends. Typical teenager, I guess."

"On the phone, or online?"

"Both, probably," Joan said. "Her laptop seemed to always be on."

"Did she ever try to hide what she was doing, if you walked in?"

"No," Joan said. "But I always knocked. She hated it if I didn't."

"Hey!" Ryan exclaimed. "So did I, but you never knocked."

"Girls need more privacy," Joan said.

"Well, that's not fair," he grumbled.

"But it's true," Sasha said, purposely using a conspiratorial tone with Joan; she was trying to keep them from worrying too much, but she was beginning to suspect that the Bartons were, as was their son, a bit too trusting that life's ugliness wouldn't descend on them.

"How on earth," Joan asked, "did a sweet girl like you get into the sad business of looking for missing children? Don't mistake me, it's wonderful and I admire you tremendously for doing it, but I'm curious."

"I got my degree and then started out working for the county, with Protective Services, but…let's just say their hands were too often tied. They'd be ordered by some judge to put a child back into a hideous home, and when that child later turned up beaten, or worse, it was just too much for me."

"Oh, dear. I can imagine."

"When I read about the Westin Foundation, I plopped myself on their doorstep until Zach Westin showed up and I literally threw myself at him. Told him I'd work for a month for free, if he'd just give me a shot. He did."

"I knew he was a smart guy," Ryan said. Sasha shot a glance at him at the implicit compliment. Ryan shrugged as if it were nothing before going on. "They say Josh himself had to step in and run the Aviation Division when he left, until they found somebody who could replace him, do everything he did. And his people would go to the wall for him, the way we all would for Josh."

"I've read about your organization," Joan said. "After we met you, we looked it up."

She slid her son a sideways glance that made Sasha wonder what Ryan's parents had thought after those brief encounters. Ryan didn't meet his mother's gaze, she noticed, and couldn't help wondering if there had been a conversation after those meetings as well. And what it had sounded like.

"So tell me, how did this become your passion?"

She supposed the fact that Joan knew this said something about what Ryan had told them. She'd been asked this before, and never hesitated to answer. It was important, she'd always thought, that people realize just how lucky they were to have the lives that they had.

"I know what it's like to lose people you love, and never know what happened to them. Most of my extended family vanished in Eastern Europe, in the darkest times in the darkest places. My grandparents risked their lives to get out. My parents and I were born here, but my family has never forgotten those we had to leave behind."

Joan's eyes widened. "Then I admire you even more, Sasha."

"Thank you, but I'm just part of a team. A great team. We—"

"She took out a thousand dollars," Patrick said grimly as he strode back into the room. "The day after her birthday."

Joan's expression of surprise told Sasha she hadn't known this either. And the expression of pained regret told her Trish's mother was feeling the weight of her perceived failure as a parent.

"Don't feel that way," Sasha said softly. "If she'd given you no reason to worry before, you can't be blamed for not seeing this coming."

"I feel like one of those clueless parents you see on television, saying they never knew their kid was into drugs, or gangs, or whatever else," Patrick muttered.

"You're not that way. Believe me, I've seen enough parents like that."

"But we are," Joan said softly. "We missed it with Ryan, too. We never realized what he was doing, hacking into the school's computer system, then the others."

"Mom," Ryan began, but when she looked at him he subsided.

"If it hadn't been for Josh Redstone, you would have ended up in jail. For who knows how long. You were just lucky he's such a generous man."

"I know that, Mom."

Ryan said it quietly, yet so intently that Sasha knew he meant every word. And she knew he did think the world of the man who had given him a chance where anyone else wouldn't have exerted himself beyond testifying to throw the kid who'd hacked his corporate security straight into a cell.

"And you should be proud of him now," Sasha said. "He's one of Redstone's finest. It's a perfect fit."

Ryan gave her a startled look at the compliment. His surprise made her wonder if she'd perhaps been too hard on him. Had she never paid him a compliment? Had she been nothing but critical? She tried to think back, but caught herself before she got lost in the morass of analysis of what had gone wrong. Right now, the thing that mattered most was finding Trish.

She hadn't thought she would have any trouble working with Ryan, despite the fact that they'd had an unsuccessful personal relationship. It had been two years ago, and it hadn't gone on very long anyway. And she wasn't finding it awkward at all, not really. But she was finding it a distraction, and one she wasn't used to; usually on a case, her focus was laser-sharp and nothing could pull her mind away from the job for long.

You weren't in the market for a geek then, and you're not now, she told herself. And that she remembered he preferred the term *tech-head* was merely irritating.

She'd lectured herself, back then, that she wanted to live life to the fullest, and hours spent in front of a computer screen didn't fit with that, not in her mind. Nor did skating along seemingly on the surface of that life, never delving deep, really understanding things. Or even trying to. Wanting to.

But she'd had to admit that she liked Ryan. A lot. And the genuine concern he was showing now for his missing sister appealed to her. A lot.

And there she was again, distracted.

"How much is the fund? Is a thousand a big chunk of it?"

"It was ten thousand," Patrick said, rubbing a hand over his face in a weary gesture Sasha had seen in almost every parent she'd dealt with over the years.

Traveling money, Sasha thought.

"She didn't clean it out," she said aloud. "That's a very good sign."

"Is it?" Joan asked, her tone hopeful.

"It suggests she plans to come back," Sasha said.

"But she could access it from any other branch of the bank that administers the trust," Patrick said.

"Yes," Sasha agreed, "but why bother? If she was there, at the bank, why not clean it out then, if she was going to do it? It's not like she'd have to carry around a wad of cash. All she'd have to do is ask for a debit card, checkbook, something like that."

Joan seemed to take heart from that, and when they finally left, even Ryan seemed relieved.

"Thanks," he said as they got back in her car. "You really made them feel better."

"I don't have a magic pill," Sasha warned.

"I know that. But you made them feel like something was being done, and that really helped."

"They're nice people."

"Yeah. Yeah, they are."

"You sound surprised."

"It's weird. They've always just been my parents, you know? But today, it was like they were...different."

"Or you saw them differently?"

He nodded slowly as she slid the key into the ignition. "I guess I never saw them as *themselves* before. People. In their own right."

"It's always a shock, to realize our parents are people, too," she said, only half teasing. "We start out as babies seeing them as merely extensions of ourselves. The first shock is when we realize they're separate."

"Good thing we can't remember that, I guess."

"What we should remember is that they were kids, and grew up feeling the same things we did, that they had dreams, and plans, felt hope and pain and joy and frustration, just like we do."

"Almost as weird as thinking about them having sex," Ryan said wryly.

Sasha laughed. "And yet here we are, living proof."

"Yeah," he said, but he was smiling, as if he was pleased that he'd made her laugh. "Now what?" he asked then.

"I want to go back to Westin," she said. "Check her Web page, see if there are any clues there. Did she have a blog?"

"I'm not sure."

"Okay, you can look for one while I check out her page and linked friends and all that."

He nodded, seemed to hesitate, then said, "Thanks," again.

"For what?"

"Letting me help."

"She's your sister, and you've got the computer smarts," she said. "I'd be crazy to turn down that help. Especially," she said, eyeing him as she pulled to a stop at the corner of the quiet, pleasant cul de sac he'd grown up on, "when we may need to do some hacking."

He blinked. "Hacking?"

"Without the weight of the police behind us, conducting an official investigation, getting permission to check, say, IM logs, or true addresses behind AKAs and screen names could be…problematic. I assume something like that is well within your fabled abilities?"

His expression was an odd combination of pride and embarrassment. "Yeah. I can do that."

"I thought so."

"You're okay with that?" he asked, clearly curious at her willingness to skirt some legalities.

"It's the joy of not working for the government. The focus is on getting the job done, not jumping through hoops and over obstacles put in our way by people who seem more focused on protecting the bad guy than saving the innocent."

"You sound like Reeve talking about why it's good to be Redstone Security."

"Same principle, I'm sure." She frowned as something hit her. "Wait, maybe you'd better not do this. I'll get somebody else. I don't want you getting in any trouble if somebody catches you. You've already got a record for that kind of thing."

He shook his head. "Josh had it expunged."

She glanced at him. "He did?"

Ryan nodded. "As a gift, on my fifth-year anniversary with Redstone." His mouth twisted wryly. "After I'd finished my punishment."

"Punishment?"

"Josh made me go teach computer classes to inmates at the county jail. His not-too-subtle message being this could be my world if I didn't straighten up."

Sasha's eyes widened. She'd thought, all this time, that Ryan had gotten off fairly lightly for what he'd done. She hadn't been sure she'd approved of that, the lack of consequences. She should have known, from what she'd heard of Josh Redstone, that he wouldn't believe in that either.

"Anyway, his guy St. John handled it. Now *there's* a guy who gets the job done."

"So I've heard. Zach's mentioned him. Said he wished he could recruit him for the foundation."

"He'd be an asset, that's for sure. The guy knows scary people in very scary places, and they all seem to owe him."

"And sometimes the kids we're looking for end up in scary places."

"Yeah."

He said it quietly, and there was a fear that was all too familiar to her in the single syllable. She'd heard it too often in her work, and she wished, for Ryan's sake as she had for others, that she had that magic pill that would put everything right. But she didn't.

And while she could work 24/7 to find her, there wasn't anything she could say that could take away a fear that was too often founded in reality.

Trish Barton could well be in a very scary place.

Chapter 7

"Was your sister unhappy?"

"Not on the surface."

Ryan answered Sasha's question as he paced the large room at the Westin Foundation, where they'd gone because there was a computer setup where they could both work. The foundation was in an old house that had been updated, yet still seemed of another era, with solid wood-paneled walls and dividers between spaces, and not a trace of modern chrome or glass.

Sasha poured over Trish's colorful Web page, complete with a long list of "friends" who had asked to be added to her list.

"Underneath?" she asked.

He let out a sigh. "I guess you know I have no idea. I should have been paying more attention."

She didn't answer that, and Ryan guessed it was because the answer was "Yes, you should have," and she didn't see the point. She'd told him in essence the same thing two years ago, that he should be more thankful for his family, and stop taking them for granted.

What she'd told his parents, about her family history, was clattering around in his mind. He'd known it, from before. Had even commented on it once, about how exotic it was to an umpteenth-generation American like himself.

"My family's history isn't exotic, you doofus," she'd snapped at him. "It's ugly. Painful. Do you know the slightest thing about real pain, Ryan?"

I do now, he thought wearily.

He had taken them for granted, assumed they'd always be there, so they weren't something he needed to bother about on a day-to-day basis. Now he knew better. And no matter how much he tried to tell himself that this was an aberration, that Trish would soon be back and everything would be back to normal, he couldn't quite sell himself on it.

And the dark-haired woman beside him was a big part of the reason why.

Since they'd parted ways, he'd tracked the Westin Foundation, telling himself it was just curiosity, not a need to know where she was and what she was doing. And when an alert came through to his e-mail, sending him to read some news article about them, he scanned it quickly for her name—which didn't appear all that often. Zach was the public face, arriving at his high profile in the field in the most painful way possible.

So he knew what she and her colleagues dealt with on a daily basis. Knew that while their success rate was astounding by official measures, that sometimes that success came too late; they found the missing child, but what they found was a shell of what had once been an innocent life.

Or what they found was a body.

Ryan suppressed the shudder that went through him. He leaned forward and made himself focus on the page on the wide-screen monitor. Nice color saturation, he thought, sharp image, and no dead pixels. He made a note of the brand; Ian Gamble needed a new one, and it was up to him to pick it out and install it—Ian would never stop his work long enough to do it.

I'm as bad as my mother, he thought, *stalling.*

He made himself read over Sasha's shoulder, dreading what he might find. But all he saw was more of why he'd avoided it in the first place.

"Besides the fact that she says she'll be away for a while, see anything that jumps out?"

"You mean besides that damned provocative picture of her in that bikini?"

"Not unusual, I'm afraid."

"Yeah, but it is for my little sister. She's not that…bold."

"It's easy to be more confident in cyberspace than you are in person. But is there anything, for instance, that you know isn't true?"

Ryan knew kids often lied on these pages, to make themselves or their lives seem more exciting. But after a few moments more of reading, he shook his head.

"Nothing outright false, just…embellished. At least the stuff I know about. Most of it I don't."

"I'll make a note to ask your parents about a couple of these things."

He shook his head as he continued to scan. "When did she turn into such a drama queen?" he asked, more to himself than to Sasha, who obviously couldn't know.

But he saw now why she'd asked if Trish was happy; if you judged by the seemingly unceasing list of complaints about her life shown here, you'd have to assume her life was a living hell.

"Hormones," Sasha said.

Ryan's mouth twisted. "I'd get slapped if I said that."

"Yes, and you'd deserve it," she said mildly.

"You want to explain that one to me?"

"Guys might be allowed to say it if you didn't carry it way too far and attribute everything a woman does that you don't like or that ticks you off to it."

"Oh." He couldn't think of anything else to say to that, and decided not to even try.

"Of course, blaming every crazy thing a guy does on testosterone poisoning is just as bad."

"Thanks," he said. "I think."

She smiled at that, then turned back to reading the page. He went back to it, too, but didn't last long.

"Girls," he muttered. Sasha glanced at him again, her dark eyes full of amusement. "Sorry," he said.

"Don't be. It even bores me after a while." She made a wry face. "I don't understand why people think they have it so rough when in reality they're so lucky."

"Because they're not dealing in reality?" Ryan suggested.

She looked startled, then thoughtful. "Very astute, Mr. Barton."

"I'm sorry you're surprised," he said, feeling weary of being thought a lightweight by this woman.

That she'd likely been right for too long was a reality he didn't want to deal with. At least, not now.

He was grateful when her cell phone rang. From her side of the conversation he deduced it was Sheila, from Safe Haven, and when Sasha gave her a fax number, he guessed she'd found Trish's note. When she disconnected, Sasha confirmed his guess.

"Emma sends her best, Sheila says," she added. "And she said to tell you if there's anything she or her husband can do to help, just ask."

With anyone else, Ryan guessed it would be just lip service. But when there was a Redstone connection, he knew it was genuine, and that if he made that request, he would get exactly what had been offered—whatever help they could provide. They were truly a family.

Family.

It hit him suddenly that perhaps he'd been appreciating one family while taking the other for granted.

He made himself lean over and pay attention to what was going on, telling himself—not without the same mental comparison to his mother—he'd deal with that later.

"You must have looked at a lot of these. It seems pretty average to me, but…"

She accepted the change of subject, since it was back to the task at hand. "It is fairly typical. Until," she said with a gesture at the screen, "here."

He looked, read from the point she indicated onward. After several weeks' worth of entries, he was frowning.

"She stopped complaining. At least about every little thing."

"Yes. After that point, her main complaint was how over-protective your parents are, something she'd mentioned before, but it was just one on her long list."

"What changed?"

"Her attitude," Sasha answered. "The real question is, why? What happened—" she scrolled back to where the change began to show "—in mid-May?"

"I don't know."

"When did she get her college acceptance letter?"

He thought for a moment, then nodded. "About then," he said. He dug out his smart phone, did a search, nodded again. "There. We all went out to dinner to celebrate on May 12. She'd just gotten her letter that week. You think that's it? Why it all changed?"

"Maybe."

"But she's so smart, and her grades were always really good, she had no reason to think she wouldn't get in. I mean, schools came looking for her."

Sasha frowned as if that had put a kink in her theory. "Still, the stress of waiting to hear may have been why she was so…snarky."

"Nice dodge of the B-word," Ryan said, earning himself a laugh. It was ridiculous, how that pleased him so much. Especially when he shouldn't be thinking about any kind of laughter, not with Trish out there somewhere, maybe in trouble.

Maybe he was the one not dealing with reality, he thought.

Sasha was still reading, and making some notes. She went for the old-fashioned way, he saw, pen and paper as she wrote down some dates and screen names.

"I should write you guys a program that would strip that stuff out of pages like this."

She stopped mid-note. "You could do that?"

He lifted a shoulder. "Sure."

"Could you make it search for names, dates, references to things?"

"Sure."

"And maybe make it sort by different parameters, like what names show up on what dates, or vice versa, that kind of thing?"

"Easy."

"Ryan Barton, I and everyone in this office would kiss you if you could do that."

"I'll pass on Russ, thanks," he said. "But you...now that I'd take."

She truly laughed then, and he realized the sound of it soothed him like nothing else had in the past week since this had started.

No, he thought suddenly, like nothing else had since the last time he'd heard that joyous sound, two years ago.

"You two are having too much fun," a stern male voice said from the doorway. Ryan whirled, wondering if he'd somehow conjured up the resident *GQ* cover boy by mentioning him. He relaxed when he saw an older man, maybe late-forties, with brown hair cut short and graying at the temples, holding some papers. The man looked pretty buff to him, and Ryan guessed anybody who let the gray in his hair fool him would pay a price.

"Hi, Frank," Sasha said, getting to her feet. She gestured at Ryan. "Ryan Barton, Frank Bedford, once one of L.A.P.D.'s finest, now, lucky for us, one of ours."

L.A.P.D. That probably explained the world-weary look in the man's eyes. Ryan held out his hand and the other man shook it firmly, but with no show of strength. But then, he supposed even an ex-cop had nothing to prove.

"Barton," the man said slowly. "Redstone?"

Ryan nodded.

"You're the tech guy, aren't you? That video enhancement, on Josh's nephew's case, right?"

Ryan nodded again.

"It's your sister who's missing?"

For a third time, Ryan nodded.

"We'll find her," Bedford said. Then, nodding toward Sasha, he added, "No one's better at it than this one."

"I know that."

The man gestured at Sasha with the papers he held. "Fax came in. I grabbed it since it was obviously the companion to the one you gave me."

Sasha nodded. "Sheila called and said she'd found it."

Bedford stepped to the desk, laid the two pages down side by side. Ryan took a quick step forward; he'd stared endlessly at the one Trish had left at home, but he hadn't seen the one she'd left at Safe Haven at all. It was a bit longer, but in tone, didn't seem to him any different.

"What's your take?" Sasha asked Bedford.

Ryan found himself holding his breath. Sasha said the guy had a knack for analyzing such things, seeing what wasn't there. But he started with what was obvious.

"They're different. Personalized to each recipient. No way to be totally certain, of course, but the indication is that they're real, not copies left by someone else."

And Ryan didn't feel a hundred per cent good about that. It was a great relief that Trish had apparently done this herself, and hadn't been carted off by some kidnapper— although they certainly weren't a likely target; they were solidly middle class, comfortable but never going to be rich by any measure. At the same time, the thought that she'd done this on purpose, just vanished for reasons her family and friends didn't know and couldn't seem to figure out, was beyond unsettling.

"Okay, so assuming she left of her own accord," Sasha said, "what else do those tell you?"

"Nothing," Bedford said.

Ryan blinked when Sasha laughed at this. "Ever the cop. Come on, Frank, this isn't L.A.P.D., you don't have to try and explain how you got there, show probable cause or make some D.A.'s case. Just give me your gut feeling."

Frank smiled, the bleakness in his eyes abating for a moment. "All right. You know all the usual disclaimers."

"I know your instincts are beyond sharp," she said. "Tell me."

"All right. First, she left of her own free will. Second, she intends to come back. Those are obviously the two most important things."

"I'll say," Ryan said on a breath of relief; there was something about this man that inspired trust. He wondered if they taught cops how to do that, or if Bedford just naturally had it.

But Sasha merely nodded, as if she'd already known that. Which, Ryan supposed, she likely had.

"Okay, now give me the good stuff," she said, with a smile at the older man.

"All right. Third, she was happy about it. Fourth, she was also scared about it. Fifth, she didn't like keeping it a secret. Sixth, she felt like the people she worked with would understand better than her folks would. Seventh, and here's where it starts getting nebulous, she hadn't done anything like this before."

"That's not nebulous," Ryan said. "She hasn't."

"Well. There you go, then," Bedford said.

"And?" Sasha prompted.

"Eighth, and more nebulous, she knew she was acting out of character, and it frightened her a little."

"She was out of her comfort zone," Sasha said slowly, and Bedford nodded.

"Ninth, and probably the most nebulous…she was excited about more than just a trip somewhere."

Ryan went still. Sheila McKay's words echoed in his head, about the feeling she'd gotten from Trish. That *there was more than just the trip she was looking forward to.*

He stared down at the second note, read it again, and then again. Finally the words burst from him.

"I get that she did this herself, voluntarily, and it says here that she'll be back and go back to work, but how the hell do you get the all the rest of that?"

"Genius," Sasha said.

Frank snorted. "Most of it's right there. The happiness, it's in the energy in the second one. She's almost gushing excitement. The fear, well, that's two-fold, first that she knows her folks are going to be upset, that's why the effort to reassure, this 'please understand I have to do this,' and second, here—" he pointed at a spot in the second note "—she says she can't believe she's doing this."

"And that's where the 'never having done anything like this before' comes in," Sasha guessed aloud.

Bedford nodded. "And that alone scared her, but it also implies, I think, that she knew this wasn't 'her' and that either bothered or worried her. Kids her age are focused a lot on who they are, finding themselves, whatever the current phrase is. And when they do something they can't explain even to themselves, contrary to what adults might think, they do know it."

It all sounded so logical when he explained it, Ryan thought. "Where'd you get the idea she didn't like keeping it a secret?" he asked.

"Here," Bedford said, pointing to a line in the Safe Haven note. "Where she swears she will tell all as soon as she can. It's in the tone of an apology."

That made sense, too, Ryan thought. Sasha was right, the guy was good.

"And that's why you think she thought the Safe Haven people would understand better than her family?" Sasha asked. "Because she told them more, and promised to tell all when she could?"

"You're getting the hang of it, girl," Bedford said.

"But what about that last thing, that you said, and Sheila

said," Ryan asked. "About her being excited about more than just a trip?"

"That," Bedford said wryly, "I can't explain. It's just a gut feel. A hunch, if you want. I don't expect you to believe it, since there's not a damn bit of concrete evidence that I'm right."

"Sure there is," Ryan said, earning him a startled glance from Sasha and a narrowed gaze from Bedford. He lifted one shoulder in a half shrug. "You're right about all the rest. That's evidence, isn't it?"

"Well, well," Bedford said. "You're smarter than I thought."

Ryan flushed, but the smile of approval Sasha gave him eased any embarrassment he was feeling.

"Thanks, Frank," Sasha said.

"You need anything more, you let me know. We're thankfully light right now."

"Let's hope it stays that way," Sasha said as the man headed for the door of her office.

Bedford stopped in the doorway and looked back at Ryan. "Reason I didn't think you were too smart?" He nodded at Sasha. "You let her get away."

He left, whistling a cheerful tune. And to Ryan's surprise, Sasha seemed flustered, avoiding his eyes.

"Don't mind him," she said. "He's just jabbing at you."

"I didn't let you get away. You left."

She did look at him then. Steadily, levelly, in that direct way that he both liked and was a tiny bit intimidated by.

"My staying would have taken changes you weren't willing to make. So did I just leave, or did you let it happen?"

Ryan blinked. He hated conundrum questions like that. He hated the vagueness of them, the hidden aspects. With a computer, it did exactly what you told it to do, no more, no less, and the biggest puzzle involved was figuring out exactly what to tell it to get what you wanted.

People were unpredictable, unique, like throwing two completely different operating systems together; they couldn't even talk to each other, let alone accomplish anything.

Sasha had already turned back to her computer monitor, as if it had been merely a rhetorical question she'd never really expected an answer to. As, perhaps, it had been.

And damn it, now he was going to be thinking about it for days.

Chapter 8

Sasha got up out of her chair, stretching muscles protesting at the long session at the computer. This was the heart of the Westin Foundation, what Zach called the "war room," because that's what he considered their work, a war against those who would do harm to innocent children. It was where they met, compared notes, compiled what they knew and tossed around possibilities, all of which were transferred to the huge whiteboard on the end wall, with different colored markers delineating what they knew, what they suspected, what could be and the things where they had no idea if they mattered. Yet. And all the connections between them.

She guessed Ryan would think it an antiquated and inefficient process, but it worked. Something about running through all their data in a group, of putting it up where they could all see it at once, together, maybe even the physical process of writing it on the whiteboard, helped them work.

But this corner of the war room, set up with several computer terminals and the latest in other electronics, courtesy of Redstone, was Ryan's world. He was utterly at home here.

"I don't know how you sit at one of these for hours on end," she said. "My eyes are crossing and my back hurts."

"I usually don't sit so still," he answered, almost absently, still focused on his own screen. At least he'd answered her this time; once or twice he'd been so intent he hadn't even heard her.

He was tracking down the screen names she gave him as she went through Trish's pages, checking other sites and doing general searches on them, a task made more complicated by people using the same name, or a variation, everywhere, and different people using similar names in other places. It was a massive undertaking, and he was grateful Trish had landed on one of the smaller networking sites.

After a brief stop for coffee out and coffee in, Sasha was pushed by his intensity to get back to it. Interesting, she thought. Usually people were telling her to slow down, but now it was he who seemed driven. She'd never pictured him like this.

Of course, it was he who had the most to lose if they didn't come up with something here.

After another hour, even Ryan was starting to flag.

"That's something else to add to the program," he muttered. "An option to search through all other social pages and databases for what it strips out of one. Automated," he added sourly as he stood up and stretched.

Sasha glanced up, realized with a little jolt that she was looking at a rather prime backside. But then, he'd always been the type she preferred, lean and wiry rather than bulky with carefully maintained muscles, like Russ.

Two years ago, it had been when she'd found herself wondering about the rest of him, when she'd felt the heat of urgency to end the speculation and find out, that she'd realized she was well on her way to falling for him.

But she'd seen too many women make disasters of their lives by rushing in, and had spent years now dealing with the fallout, both from inexperienced young girls who had been fooled into thinking infatuation was love, or women who should have known better making lousy choices where their own children paid the price.

She was neither of those, she'd told herself firmly then. And she'd walked away.

But she'd never forgotten.

But you'd better forget now, she chided herself. *Focus, woman. What is* with *you?*

"That would be great, if you could come up with that program," she said.

There was a moment's lag time when he looked a little puzzled, and she wondered just how long she'd been lost in her own thoughts since he'd said that. But after a moment he simply answered.

"I can. I will. I'd do it now, so we could use it, but it would take too long to get it tweaked and working."

"I understand. But just the thought of having something like that to do this kind of work for us makes my back feel better."

"I thought you didn't like computers," he said, turning to face her.

"I never said that," Sasha answered, a little sharply. "They're tools, wizard tools. In a way, they can be weapons, too. In the right hands, like ours, they're one of the best in our arsenal for good. In the wrong hands, they can be devastating."

He blinked. "I never thought of it like that."

"Our job would be immensely harder without them. Our lives would be harder without them—or easier, depending on how they're working. But they shouldn't *be* our lives."

He sighed, and looked away, and Sasha knew it was the unspoken equivalent of "Here we go again."

And he'd be right. They'd had this discussion before. And this was not the time, place or circumstance to have it again. It didn't matter anyway. She'd walked away when it was clear he wouldn't change. No matter how much she liked him, no matter how much she was attracted to him, she couldn't imagine a long-term relationship with somebody who seemed to skate along so easily on the surface of life.

But she'd gotten something out of it.

Now she understood how some of those women ended up making those lousy choices.

"I think we have to consider another possibility," Sasha said briskly, gesturing at the screen that still held Trish's brightly colored page, with her list of "friends" running down a column on the right side, apparently to indicate they were back to work.

"What?" he asked, thinking he should be thankful they were out of that personal minefield. He hated that kind of discussion, and nothing made his stomach churn more than the girl of the moment telling them they needed to "talk." So why was he standing here wishing they could thrash this out, get past it, find some common ground between them?

"It's true her attitude changed about the time she got her college acceptance. So maybe it was just stress over that that had her so…"

"Bitchy?" Ryan suggested, accepting the shift back to work; he shouldn't have been thinking about anything but Trish anyway.

"Well, yes. That, and being a teenager."

"That'll do it. But you think there's something else going on?"

"Take going off to college out of it. If you read her posts and looked at the pictures and things added since that time, looked at all that cold, without knowing anything else and saw the change, what would you think?"

"That I'm glad I don't have to deal with teenage girls anymore?"

He saw her mouth twitch, but she wasn't distracted. She'd been lost in thought a while ago, but now she was back on the scent, and as intense as he remembered. It had been one of the things that had drawn him. Her passion for what she did had been incredibly attractive.

"In a way, you're right."

"Huh?"

"If I didn't know what I know, if I just read this cold, I'd think she met someone."

"Met…you mean as in a guy?"

Sasha nodded. "She started sounding like a girl in love. Or on her way to it."

"Trish?" he said, incredulous.

"It's just a feeling."

"Like Bedford's hunch?"

"Yes. And like him, I have no real evidence."

"Just the instincts that make you so good at this."

She blinked, looking startled. "Yes. Nothing I can point to, nothing these—" she gestured widely at the bank of computers "—could come up with."

She said it as if she expected him to discredit the idea because of that. He spent a moment wondering if he'd really come across that way two years ago, as if he thought computers could do everything.

Then he realized it didn't matter. What mattered was how he came across here and now.

"But this one," he said, reaching out to gently tap the side of her head, "did."

She drew back slightly, clearly not certain how to take that comparison.

"Isn't that what it is? You've built up a database in years of doing this, and you're drawing on it, looking for similarities, matches, to come up with possibilities."

Her eyes widened, and he knew he'd struck a chord. Encouraged, he went on.

"Somebody said once that if the technology doesn't seem like magic, it's not advanced enough. And you do this so fast, and make these leaps, that it seems like that kind of magic."

A smile played around the corners of her mouth. "Did you just say I'm faster than a speeding computer?"

He chuckled, glad she'd taken it that way. Progress, he thought. And he'd always admired, even been fascinated, by the way her agile mind worked. If you could build a computer to work that way, to make the kind of intuitive leaps she did, you'd really have something, he thought now.

"Sort of," he answered. "But more that your 'feeling' and Bedford's 'hunch' are likely just as founded in empirical data, but a good human brain can...skip a few steps a computer can't."

"Do I need a red pen to mark the day?"

"The day?"

"The day Ryan Barton admitted a computer can't replace a human brain."

So much for progress.

"I've never thought that," he said, weary of the argument that had been going on most of his life. "After all, the human brain thought up computers. All they do is do things faster, in more depth and with greater accuracy. Until they learn to learn, that's all they'll ever do."

She looked thoughtful then. "And you think they will, someday? Learn to learn, I mean?"

"Artificial Intelligence? Yes, they will."

"And that doesn't bother you?"

"It's a natural progression."

"And there we are," Sasha said softly. "You see progress, I see...a *Terminator* scenario."

"That's because you're a pessimist."

She blinked. "What?"

"You're always looking for the dark side." He glanced around the room. "Doing what you do, how could you not?"

For one of the few times since he'd known her, she looked as if she didn't know what to say. And at this point, neither did he.

"We've been through this before. We should get back to work," he said, rather abruptly. "You really think she...fell for this guy online?"

Sasha seemed glad of the switch. "I think there's something to the idea. All of a sudden the world was a brighter, more colorful, happier place. And if, as you said, her getting into her choice of schools wasn't that doubtful, maybe it wasn't simply getting accepted that changed her outlook."

"Damn," Ryan muttered.

"That's also about the time that 'SadBreeze' appeared on her friends list. And they exchanged a lot of public posts that got a bit more than casual before they suddenly stopped."

He'd seen that, had registered the name and wondered, but because they'd stopped, he hadn't gone beyond that. But Sasha's phrasing made him realize he should have.

"Public…you mean you think they went private?" He could think of several reasons a communication like that would go underground, and he didn't like any of them. "You think they got even more personal? Starting saying things they didn't want the whole world to see?"

"Maybe. She kept chatting with others publicly, including some guys, but this guy suddenly vanished. Did you check his page?"

"Yeah, but I didn't spend a lot of time," Ryan said, turning back to his own keyboard and calling it back up.

"When did he show up?"

Ryan checked. "About a year ago. A month after Trish."

"Does he talk about where he lives?"

He vaguely remembered a photo of the Space Needle, but checked the profile before saying, "It says near Seattle. Across Puget Sound."

"What's he look like?"

Ryan blinked. "I don't know. A guy. Dark hair, kind of tall, I guess, judging by this pic with his buddies."

Sasha leaned over to look. "Killer grin," she observed. "Pretty cut, too. Tan, sparkly teeth…very cute. Yeah, a teenage girl would be ripe for that."

She said it with such detachment it almost amused him. Almost. "It says he's got dogs, and a horse. So they'd have that in common."

Sasha scanned the entries, the pictures and captions. Stopped at one of a lolling pair of Golden Retrievers and read it aloud, "'I know it's way too emo, but I love my dogs. They're the coolest.' Nice touch, the sheepish embarrassment about a tender feeling. Very masculine, but guaranteed to melt any girl's heart."

Ryan's mouth quirked. "If only I'd known."

Sasha flashed him a quick smile, the tension between them apparently forgotten now they were back on the hunt.

"The posts he left on her page said he found her because he searched for people who liked what he liked, and they had everything in common."

"Looks like they do," Ryan said.

"Or he wanted her to think they do. She was pretty open on her page."

"Meaning?"

"His page came after hers. He could have set it up to mirror hers. Lure her in with the similarities, make her think she'd met her soul mate."

"You mean he set it all up? That's a bit extreme, isn't it? After all, the whole purpose of these sites is to meet people with like interests, right?"

"But you're not meeting them actually *doing* those things. You only have what they say to go by."

"But to set up a whole page just to get one girl to think you have stuff in common?"

"It happens. And at that age, when this started, girls are very vulnerable. Their emotions are confused and complicated. It makes them easy prey."

"Prey?" He didn't like the sound of that.

"They think they're getting romance, someone who really cares about them, who wants to know them, and be with them forever. What they're really getting is some jerk of a guy looking for no-strings sex."

No strings, that's the way for me....

His own thought flashed through his mind, jolting him. He shifted uncomfortably, glad that her lightning-quick brain hadn't progressed to being able to read his mind. She was worried Trish had run into someone intent on only one thing. Someone who wanted not a long-term commitment, but care-free, heart-free, un-entangled sex.

Someone like him.

Damn, he muttered to himself.

He didn't like the thought of being like some teenage Romeo. He wondered if Sasha had meant the observation as a jab at him, told himself he was doing it again, making it all about him. It didn't help much.

He should have known. He should have known this would happen. She would toss his life into turmoil.

She always had.

Distracted, he only belatedly arrived at where Sasha already had.

"You think she's gone to meet him? This kid?"

"Let's hope."

He blinked. "What? You want her to have taken off to meet some kid she met online?"

"I meant, let's hope it's a kid. That he's for real."

His brow furrowed. "What do you mean?"

"I mean that he's acted exactly like a horny kid who's out to seduce some impressionable young girl."

He managed not to wince at the unflattering portrait, given his own recent thoughts. "And?"

"That's also the way many Internet predators operate."

"Internet preda—"

He broke off as her meaning hit home. Hard. "God, I'm an idiot," he breathed. "How could that not be the first thing I thought of? Me, of all people?"

"Your emotions are involved," Sasha said gently. "Nobody thinks clearly when their emotions are in high gear."

"But it's my work! I should have—"

"You would have. Eventually. You know how they set up an entire false front, a persona, incredibly detailed. All a mask for who they really are."

Ryan felt a queasiness in the pit of his stomach. The thought of Trish being talked into hooking up with some kid she'd never laid eyes on before was one thing. The thought of his little sister in the hands of some pervert who used networks like this to lure girls was something else altogether.

"That's one of the things I meant," Sasha added quietly, "when I said sometimes computers can be weapons. Or, I suppose, traps. Snares."

He wanted to smash something. And the computer sitting there glowing, tempting, was the best target he could see.

Snares. His beloved computers. Trish.

No matter what happened, he knew nothing was ever going to be the same for him.

Chapter 9

"We've already gone through all her cell phone bills. There are no strange numbers, just the usual," Ryan said. "And I tried a GPS trace, but it's not registering."

"She may have not actually talked to the guy. It's not uncommon for the whole thing to be conducted online."

Especially if the guy isn't who he says he is and knows his voice will give him away, Ryan thought, his stomach knotting once more. He tried to quash it by asking his next question.

"If she paid cash for an airplane ticket, how do we find out if that's really where she went?" He gave Sasha a sideways look as she dialed a number on her cell. "Short of hacking into the airline Web sites, that is. Not that I couldn't do it, but it's kind of frowned on these days."

"It was always frowned on," Sasha said, as blandly as if he'd been talking about stealing a drink from a public water fountain. "It's just that today there are teeth behind the frown."

"Then what do we—"

He stopped when she held up a hand.

"Lauren? Sasha Tereschenko. Yes, it has been a while, but that's good, isn't it?"

There was a pause, then Sasha laughed. "Yes. How is that darling little girl of yours?"

She listened, apparently to a gushing mother, before getting down to business. Ryan tried to rein in his impatience. But he could tell by the change in her tone when she shifted gears.

"I need the usual. Except this one's personal." Ryan liked that she felt that way. "I know without the police involved and a warrant you can't tell me specifically what I need to know, but can I tell you what I think and you tell me if I'm right? Or at least tell me if I'm warm, so I don't waste precious time in the wrong skies, so to speak?"

Ryan was still working that one out when Sasha went on.

"One week ago, on Tuesday. Trish Barton. Southern California airport, probably John Wayne, to Seattle." There was another pause. "I know it's a pain when there are so many possible airports, but I think O.C. is a good bet." A pause again. "Thanks, Lauren. And send me a photo of that kidlet."

When she'd hung up, Ryan lifted a brow at her.

"Lauren Shepherd. She used to be a travel agent, now she's on an FAA committee. She's worked with us before."

"They let her do this kind of check?"

"Usually it's the police who come at her with a warrant or the promise of one, and we're just the liaison. But Lauren would do anything for Westin, and for Zach."

She seemed to hesitate. He just waited for her to go on. She seemed surprised, but then she'd always said patience had never been his strong suit. Finally she answered.

"Zach found her little girl, when she was taken by a sex offender neighbor. And he found her before the creep had the chance to do anything. Lauren or her husband would probably kill for Zach if need be."

He had the feeling she meant that quite literally.

"She's good," Sasha added reassuringly. "If Trish is there to be found, she'll find her."

"What if she doesn't?"

"Then we try something else."

"And what if we can't find anything else? What if she really just vanished?"

Sasha eyed him with an odd sort of intentness. "And tell me, mister sunshine, when did you become a pessimist?"

After you walked out of my life, he almost said.

"This is my little sister," he managed to say instead.

"Yes," Sasha said gently, "it is."

Her mouth curved just slightly upward. He wondered what the hell there was to smile about. Especially when confronted with the possibility that Trish had been lured by some twisted, dirty old man posing as a teenager. He knew it happened, he'd just never expected it to happen to anyone he knew.

Let alone someone he loved.

Sasha continued her perusal of Trish's page while she waited for Lauren to return her call. She knew the woman had picked up on the urgency in her voice, knew that she would set all else aside for the time it took to get her answer. She'd meant what she'd told Ryan; Lauren or Mike Shepherd would probably risk anything for Westin and Zach. So they were always careful not to ask too much, or push her for anything that would get her in trouble.

The more she looked at the page, the more she was convinced she was on the right track. There was just something…giddy about the tone of Trish's entries after she and SadBreeze had been exchanging comments for about a month. Even the entries that weren't to him, or about him, held that same excitement, as if the endorphins of falling in love had spilled over into all aspects of her life and outlook.

Not that she knew from firsthand experience. She didn't. She'd never been in love like that. Maybe it went hand in hand with that pessimism Ryan accused her of.

You're always looking for the dark side. Doing what you do, how could you not?

His words came back to her then. They had been fairly perceptive. Yet another apparent change in a guy who before had rarely even thought about the way people reacted, let alone why.

When her cell rang, the quiet, discreet ring she'd chosen to be the least disturbing to frantic parents, she grabbed it quickly.

"Lauren?"

"You're in friendly skies, Sasha. Your bird definitely flew."

"Bless you, Lauren."

"Oh, no. You have that backward."

When she disconnected the call and closed her phone, she turned to look at Ryan. He looked like he was holding his breath.

"We were right. She flew to Seattle."

He let out the breath. "You were right."

He spoke the correction mildly, but she appreciated the distinction. Or rather, that he'd felt compelled to make it; she didn't care who got the credit as long as the job got done.

"Now what?" he asked, clearly deferring to her expertise.

"First, we need to find out everything we can about this guy. If he's who he purports to be, then we may have some time. If he's not…"

His jaw tightened, and she knew he understood. If they were dealing with a simple teenage romance, or even some more nefarious kind of teenage game, that was one thing.

Dealing with an adult masquerading as a teen for his own evil purposes was something else entirely.

"Is this where I come in?" he asked, his voice nearly as tight as the muscles of his jaw.

"It would go a lot quicker than if I tried," Sasha said. "But I don't want to get Westin in trouble."

"Since what I'm about to do isn't exactly by the book?"

She looked at him levelly. "Yes. Problem?"

"It's my sister. No problem." He stood up abruptly. "And you're right, I don't want you, or this place, to get into any trouble. I'll do it from my place. I have a couple of programs on my computer that might help."

She stood up then as well, glad to be moving. "Let's go."

He went still for a moment, clearly nonplussed. At the mere idea of her setting foot in his inner sanctum? She never had, before. She knew where he lived—if he was in the same place—but she'd never been inside.

"All right," he finally said.

Face it, she reminded herself as they headed back outside to the courtyard parking area, *you were too hot for him to trust yourself to go home with him.*

Besides, it would only have confirmed her suspicions, she was sure. It would be so full of his beloved computers and nothing else, and that would have depressed her.

But now, it didn't matter anymore. And now, the more and better computer equipment he had, the better for their purpose: finding Trish.

She was aware of his easy stride as they walked. She'd not been surprised to learn he'd had some skill as an athlete, being a promising baseball player before the lure of computers had overtaken him.

"Do you ever play baseball anymore?"

He looked startled. "I... Yeah, now and then. Some guys from Redstone get together and take on some other guys, just for fun."

"Good," she said, not sure why she cared. So not sure that she quickly changed the subject. "Do you want to go by and pick up your car from The Grill and take it home, then I'll follow?"

He nodded. "Good idea."

They made the drive back to the popular restaurant in relative silence. Ryan sat staring out the front, his fingers tapping restlessly on the armrest as if he were already at his keyboard. She stayed quiet, assuming he was planning his approach, if that's how you did such things. She was competent with computers, in that she could get what she wanted and needed done, could hook up peripherals and get them to work, and had even helped a girlfriend set up a wireless network, but she knew Ryan was on a whole different level.

When they got to The Grill, he directed her to the side of the building, where the locals knew to park because the building itself provided shade in the afternoons, critical in the heat of a Southern California summer. She was a little surprised when he pointed at a bright blue PT Cruiser.

"New car?"

He shrugged. "I have to lug around equipment sometimes. It's easer than having to switch back and forth to a Redstone truck or van all the time."

"Cute," she said, wondering why he winced at the word. "Are you still in the same apartment?"

"No. I've got a condo down off Coast Highway. You can follow me." She wasn't sure what her expression had been, but he grimaced. "Don't look so shocked. A guy can't live in a tiny apartment forever." He shot her a sideways look before adding, "Besides, I needed more room for my computers. You know, my only friends?"

"I never said that!"

"Bet you thought it, though."

She had, in her more sour moments, even knowing it wasn't strictly true. "I knew you had friends," she said. "I just wasn't sure you had any that didn't live and breathe computers."

"A couple," he said. "Now I have more."

She wondered if that was a jab. Told herself it didn't matter, because if it was she probably had it coming. It seemed Ryan had grown up a bit in the past two years. It didn't seem that long a time, and she herself didn't think she was that much different than she had been, but she'd always heard it happened later for guys, the maturing thing.

She'd also heard that for some, it never happened at all. She'd pretty much put Ryan in that category when she'd walked away from him. Now she was wondering if maybe she'd been a little hasty. He seemed different, in some ways at least.

He drove toward the ocean with a bit of urgency but no reck-lessness, she noticed, changing lanes to gain some speed now and then in the coastal traffic, but not crazily. He was in a hurry, but wanted to get there alive.

She was surprised when they turned into a newer, slightly upscale two-story complex set on a hill that had a partial view of the Pacific over the tops of the buildings below. It wasn't one of those luxury places, but it was better than nice.

She caught his gesture as he pointed at a series of unmarked spaces labeled guest parking, in a gap between the series of in-dividual garages they were driving along. She flipped on her turn signal to show him she understood, and pulled into one of the empty spaces.

She picked up the folder of things she'd printed out from Trish's page, things she hadn't gone through yet. She'd brought them figuring she'd go through them while Ryan was…doing whatever it was he was going to do.

"You sure you want to be a witness to this?"

He'd come up beside her as she was hitting the button to lock her car.

"If it gets the job done, let them come after me."

It wasn't until they were walking into the complex that he spoke again. Sasha was noticing the lush landscaping, lots of flowering plants and the ubiquitous palm trees, but arranged as if the buildings had been carefully placed among them and not the other way around. It was a nice touch, and she liked it.

"So you're an any-means-to-the-end person?"

She heard no censure, only curiosity in his voice, so she answered him without heat. "I know some people feel nothing justifies that. I think they're wrong. There's too little innocence left in this world, and it should be protected. Not the people who want to destroy it."

He stopped beside a stairway, and turned to face her. "You're as passionate about this as you ever were," he said.

"The day I'm not, it will be time to quit."

"Then you'll never quit."

Startled, Sasha stood stock-still for a moment as he started up the stairs. Because he was right. She would never quit. Because nothing could change how she felt about this. It was too deeply ingrained in her.

It wasn't the assessment that startled her; she'd known that about herself for a long time. It was that Ryan knew it. Had she underestimated him before?

She started after him, up the stairs. Caught herself admiring the way he moved. And watching the backside she'd had brought to her attention earlier. Definitely prime.

Some things, she thought wryly, hadn't changed at all.

Chapter 10

When she stepped inside the condo, Sasha nearly stopped in her tracks, stunned. It wasn't the spaciousness of the great room design. It wasn't the granite counters and stainless steel in the kitchen she could see off to the right. It wasn't even the lovely view out the floor-to-ceiling window on the ocean side of the room, although it was indeed stunning.

The place was immaculate. Well, to her eyes, anyway. Having grown up with her mother's possessive clutter, her criteria might be a bit skewed. And now that she looked closer, she saw a couple of books here, a stack of magazines—how many computer magazines were there, anyway?—there, and a sweatshirt tossed over the back of the couch. There was a sizable but not huge flat-screen TV fitted into a niche that seemed designed for it, so that it didn't seem to dominate the entire room.

And while he had taken refuge in the male safe zone of earth tones, dark tan leather sofa and two matching chairs, a solid coffee table with storage and a geometric patterned rug on the wood floor, there were some surprises there, too. A bright yellow knitted throw was a slash of color thrown over the back of one end of the sofa.

My favorite color, she thought. *And I am so not even going there. My ego's not that huge.*

She continued looking around. There was, even more surprisingly, a strikingly shaped, tall glass vase in the same yellow shade on one of the bookshelves built in on each side of the gas-log fireplace. The final touch hung over the mantel—a painting, a beach scene at sunset, with colors so vivid in the sky that the ocean seemed almost an afterthought. Here again were streaks of the same bright yellow. And those three splashes of color pulled the whole place out of bachelor pad and into…she wasn't sure what.

A woman's touch? she wondered. Had some girlfriend helped him with this, and was she still in the picture? Was it really coincidence, this choice of color?

She wasn't going to ask, she told herself firmly.

Ryan turned from where he'd tossed his keys on a table just inside the door. There was a racklike piece on the table as well, with an odd assortment of cables sticking out of different slots, and it took her a moment to realize it was a charging station for a cell phone and other electronics. Clever, she thought. And pure Ryan. No girlfriend behind that one, she guessed.

"My compliments to your decorator."

The words were out before she could stop them. And telling herself she hadn't actually asked didn't help much.

"What?"

"It's a great space," she said, figuring that was neutral enough.

"I like it." He walked over to the granite-surfaced bar on the room side of the kitchen island. "I was kind of iffy about actually buying a place, but Mac convinced me it was one of the best things to do. And you don't tell Mac McClaren no when he tells you what to do with your money."

"I would think not," Sasha said. "And if you could afford this, he's obviously advised you well."

She looked around again. She knew Redstone paid well, but she made a decent amount at the foundation—in a way also thanks to Redstone—and she was in no way close to being able to do something like this. She'd been in her own apartment for nearly five years now, and while she lived comfortably, it wasn't her own space, not like this.

"He'd probably help you, too, if you wanted. You're part of Redstone, in a way."

Startled, she turned back to him. How had he known what she was thinking? How had he known she was feeling as if she'd somehow fallen behind? She'd always lectured him about being a grown-up and thinking about more than just living in the moment—rather pompously, she had to ruefully admit now—and yet it was now he who'd managed this.

"He'd have to have something to work with first," Sasha said.

Ryan studied her for a moment. "Still helping your folks?"

"No, not anymore," she said. "I only did in the beginning because I talked them into that house. After all, my dad didn't want to spend the money even if the old one was falling down. Business is better now, so they're doing fine. But we had to move my grandmother into a new place, so I'm helping with that."

And while yes, that was where a sizable amount of her income went, it didn't account for all of it. There was money left, but she hadn't done much with it, and she was feeling at the moment that she'd fallen down on planning for her own future.

"You've done well, Ryan," she said. "I should apologize for all the times I accused you of never thinking beyond today."

He leaned back against the bar, looking at her steadily. "Don't. Maybe that's why I finally did it."

Her brows rose as he startled her again.

"You were right about a lot of things, Sasha. Not all, but a lot."

"I was…arrogant and supercilious," she said.

Ryan laughed. "And you've still got a killer vocabulary."

He was so obviously teasing she couldn't help but smile, but she also noticed he didn't deny her self-accusation. But then, how could he, when it was true? Even if she had been right about a lot of things, she'd been a bit too smugly superior in her criticisms. She'd always thought he had been the one who needed to change. But now, in the space of a single day, she'd come to see that she'd had some learning to do herself.

He moved then, nodding toward the hallway that ran off one end of the great room. "Computer room is back here."

She followed him, pausing only to let her fingers trail over the knitted throw; it was as soft to the touch as it looked.

"I like it," she said when he glanced back at her.

"Trish gave it to me. I liked the way it looked. She said I should get a couple more things, so I did."

"It looks great."

"Your color," he said, and headed down the hall.

Sasha went after him, pondering the answer she'd gotten to part of her unasked question; he knew perfectly well it was her favorite color. But it was a stretch to think anything as stupid as he'd chosen it for that reason.

Sure, he's been pining away all this time, putting bits of your favorite color in his home to remind him of you. That's it, sure.

She smiled at her own self-deprecation, thinking she'd beaten that bit of egocentric thought into submission.

As they went down the hallway she saw a closed door to her left. Master bedroom, she guessed, given that it likely had a similar view of the ocean in the distance that the main space had. She stifled the tiny nudge of curiosity that wanted to rise to the surface, about what kind of bedroom he would have.

Another place you're so not going, she chided herself, almost fiercely.

On the right was a bathroom, which he pointed out in case she needed it as they went past the doorway. A glance showed the same workmanship as the rest of the condo, although the counter here looked like some kind of textured stone tiles rather than the smooth polished granite of the kitchen counters.

In what was obviously intended as a second bedroom, Sasha found what she'd expected to find in the rest of the place—the lair of a terminal computer geek. A workstation against one wall, with two side-by-side wide-screen monitors, three printers, and a couple of things she didn't immediately recognize, dominated the room. There were shelves around the rest of the room that held books, software and hardware boxes, CD jewel cases and sound-system speakers.

On the wall in one of the few bare spaces was a poster that startled her. It was a vintage scene of the World War II era, a recruitment poster of sorts, with an army-green bomber emblazoned with the symbol of America, flying over what was apparently supposed to be Big Ben in London. Across the bottom, in letters three inches high, were the words, "They've done their part, now it's our turn!"

Curious, she turned to look at Ryan.

"It's a game I play. World War II based. I know how you feel about them, but—"

He stopped when she shook her head. "Is it based on the real history?"

"Yeah." Then, with a crooked grin, "I'm about to liberate France."

"All right, then. And if it makes you think for a moment about why they fought, all the better."

He looked at her for a silent moment before saying, almost sadly, "You still don't do anything just for fun?"

"You don't have fun playing that game?" she countered.

"That's not the point." The look in his eyes was almost weary, and Sasha found it strangely unsettling.

For the first time since she'd told him that there was no future for them, Ryan thought she might have been right. That even the good times they'd had together had seemed transient even in the midst of them; he'd always sensed she was on some level thinking about her work, eager to get back to it. But when her work was what it was, complaining about it seemed not just whiny, but selfish. But he'd wanted to complain. Had wanted her all to himself, at least sometimes.

Which only made his confusion deeper. He hadn't even wanted "a future," not in the way women meant it, so why had that bothered him so much?

At least, he hadn't wanted it then.

Now?

He didn't know. And he didn't have time to think about it now. His future would be pretty grim anyway if they didn't find Trish.

He sat down at the keyboard. Ian Gamble's wife, the extra-hot Samantha, had once told him he was like a concert pianist, producing near miraculous things. It was only his instrument that was different. He'd preened over that for weeks, wishing there was another woman like her out there—gorgeous, sexy, smart and appreciative of his skills.

Of course, that she was also one of the toughest, most capable of Redstone's vaunted security team added an extra kick to her repertoire, even if she had been temporarily sidelined by pregnancy.

"How do you start?" For the first time since he'd known her Sasha sounded self-conscious. As if she were talking only to break a silence that she was uncomfortable with. One of the things he'd liked about her was that she didn't have the need to fill every silent moment with chatter; this was different enough that he noticed.

"First I look for anybody else who's gotten into that particular site. See if they've bragged about it, and how they did it."

"They do that?"

"Hackers are a proud bunch," he said, starting his search with forums that might document a hack, and blogs that might crow about one.

"Were you?"

He gave her a sideways glance. "Yeah. I was."

"If you got into Redstone, you must have been good."

He lifted one shoulder in a half shrug. "I still am."

He heard her reaction, a quick intake of breath, rather than saw it, since he was focused on the results of his initial search on the screen. And suddenly he felt the need to explain, something he hadn't felt in a long time.

"I swore to Josh that I would never hack another system unless Redstone asked me. I've kept that promise."

"And has Redstone asked?"

"A time or two." Once John Draven, the legendary head of security, had called him in. "I actually hacked a hacker trying to get into the Aviation Division system, a guy who was after Josh's design for the Hawk V."

"Industrial spying?"

"Yeah. It was kind of exciting," he admitted.

"I hope you found him."

"I did. He hadn't gotten anything beyond the artist's conception yet."

"Good. If people like that would put half the energy into doing something legitimate, they'd be successful and wouldn't have to try and steal someone else's work."

Ryan smiled wryly. "I've heard that song before."

And he had; it had been the standard refrain from the moment he'd been found out, from everyone, parents, cops, counselors, all of them. But only Josh had given him the chance and the technology to do just that.

"Have they ever asked you to…cross the line?"

His head whipped around. "Of course not!" He nearly snapped it, at the very idea. "This is Redstone, and if you knew anything about Josh, you'd know he doesn't play the game that way. Not that he isn't ruthless when he has to be, but he has his own rules and he lives and works by them. As do all of us, or we don't stay Redstone for long."

"I just wondered what kind of things you've been called on to do for them."

He hesitated, then accepted the explanation. "It varies.

Mostly I work in R&D, but once I even did a job for knows all, sees all, never sleeps St. John."

"What did he want you to do?"

"To backtrack a virus." He didn't say that the virus nearly caused havoc before it had been stopped by the defenses he himself had installed on the Redstone systems; it sounded a bit like bragging. "And then turn it back on its creator."

She lifted a brow. "That sounds like quick justice."

"That's what it felt like, too," he agreed.

Mutating that worm and sending it off to destroy the destroyer had given him a sense of satisfaction he'd never felt before. Sort of like how cops must feel, he had thought, when they put away the really bad guys for life.

Or maybe like Sasha felt, when she found a child safe and sound.

Interesting, he thought now as he dug deeper through his results, going from link to link, setting items of interest aside on the second monitor for later reference. He hadn't remembered until now that he'd made that connection. It must be just that she was here, beside him, that had the old memories and feelings stirring.

He'd found a thread that looked promising, a series of posts and blog entries at an underground site he'd once frequented, that gave him a clue to a vulnerability. He zeroed in on one poster, who had claimed success. He felt the old exhilaration building; this had been his life once, this kind of surreptitious hunting down of weaknesses, all of it tinged with a kind of scorn for those less versed than he in this electronic world.

And now he stood against them, for the man who'd given him the chance to make good. And it gave him the same kind of thrill. Better, in fact, because he, like the rest of Redstone, would walk over hot coals, broken glass or anything else for Josh. As his reaction to Sasha's relatively innocent question had proven.

Out of the corner of his eye he saw her make a note on a page and reach for her cell to make a call. He glanced at her, wondering if she really believed that he cared about nothing but computers. He could even admit to himself now that he could see why she'd thought that, two years ago. Maybe he had been a bit out of balance. But his life was so much bigger now, so much wider, thanks to Redstone. Why, Josh had even sent him on a world tour, to take his security programs and ideas to Redstone facilities all over the globe. Unlike Trish, content to stay at home, he'd jumped at the chance.

Especially since the chance had come just after Sasha had dumped him. And he had had a great time. Had spent six weeks traveling in style on the Hawk III, being welcomed as a representative of Redstone, with all that entailed.

And while he'd worked hard, he'd also played hard, telling himself he didn't care a bit about the intense, too-serious woman he'd left behind. He'd even believed it, for the duration of the trip. It was only when he'd returned home that he'd had to admit it had only been a diversion. And that he—

A line in a post by that same hacker who had claimed success caught his eye. It started something stirring in his mind, an approach, a possible way in.

"There you are," he murmured, leaning forward, all other thoughts and conversation forgotten.

He was closing in.

Chapter 11

Sasha watched Ryan, sensing he was oblivious to her at the moment. She understood that kind of intensity, she had it herself when she was on a case. And she realized she'd never seen him at work before. Had never seen him turn the concentration that had seemed to her overkill when he was playing some game, to what she thought of as a useful task. She'd accused him of always wanting to play, of never taking anything seriously, but she'd done it having never really seen him work. If she'd seen this, would she have felt differently?

If she'd seen this, would she have dismissed him so quickly?

If she'd seen this, would she have left at all?

You've done well, Ryan. I should apologize for all the times I accused you of never thinking beyond today.

Don't. Maybe that's why I finally did it.

Their exchange came back to her with a jolt. Could that be even a little true, that her chiding—okay, face it, nagging—had prodded him to change?

The questions came at her like a barrage in his war game. She stared down at the printouts she'd brought with her, not seeing the words on the page, but instead lost in the memories of two years ago, wondering, questioning herself in a way she'd not done in a long time.

She'd always thought of herself as confident, certain, sure of her path and the rightness of it. And she still was, when it came to her work. But at the moment, she wasn't nearly so sure she'd trod the right path in her personal life.

You still don't do anything just for fun?

Ryan's question gnawed at her harder than her own.

Of course she had fun, she told herself. She had friends, she went out, went to movies, the occasional party. Why, she'd had a great time at the birthday party Zach had thrown for Reeve, and a better time at their wedding, and even Frank Bedford and his wife threw a mean barbecue, and of course there were often parties given by grateful families....

Her thoughts trailed away as another realization struck. She concentrated, but finally gave up the effort with a grimace. Other than the occasional movie or lunch with a girlfriend, almost all of her social outings were somehow work-related.

He was right. Apparently she never did anything just for fun, even though she had fun doing many things. It was a fine line, true, but she couldn't deny he had a point.

"Gotcha," Ryan muttered at his screen.

She dropped the file of papers onto the floor and leaned over to look. "You found him?"

"Not him, exactly. Not yet. But the account used to set up his page, and the ISP he uses, are both based in Washington."

"So near Seattle's probably the truth."

"Looks like it."

"So if we take that list of the places he mentioned going to, we might be able to narrow down a search area."

"But some of them are local names for places. I don't think you'll find just 'the creek' on a map anywhere."

She nodded. "We'll have to find a local, then."

He looked thoughtful, then glanced at his watch. That was an addition, she thought suddenly; he'd not worn one when they'd been together, but had relied on his cell phone if he needed to know what time it was. She wondered why the change, but that curiosity vanished when he went for the cell phone next and dialed quickly.

"Hi, Tam," he said when the call was answered. "Ryan Barton, from R&D." There was a pause while the other person responded. "Yeah, still looking for her. Thanks, I appreciate it."

Sasha gathered from that that the people at Redstone knew about his search. She supposed he'd had to tell them to explain his absence.

"We have a facility up near Seattle, right?"

He waited, listening intently before speaking again.

"I need somebody who's been there a while. Long enough to know the local hot spots, and names for them. Places where maybe kids would hang, you know, teenagers."

Another pause as he listened, longer this time, and then, "Yeah, that'd be great."

With a couple of quick keystrokes he opened up what appeared to be a notepad of some kind on his screen, designed to look like, of all things, a sticky note. He typed in the number the person was obviously giving him, then added a name. Rand Singleton.

"Yeah, we think she went up there. We're trying to narrow it down to exactly where. Then I'll be heading up there."

She'd wondered about that, if he'd want to go himself. If it were her, wild buffalo couldn't keep her from it, but she hadn't been certain about Ryan.

"Okay. I appreciate it."

He thanked the person on the other end and flipped his phone closed.

"A local?" she asked, indicating the note.

"Better," he said. "A local who's also Redstone Security."

"So this Rand guy will help?"

"I'm Redstone, he's Redstone. He'll help. Tam is going to call him, let him know what's going on."

"Tam?"

"Tamara Hunter. She's new. Well, not to Redstone, but to this job. Sort of a facilitator. Josh wanted somebody dedicated to just handling employee situations. Said he didn't want to take the chance that somebody who needed help didn't get it because they were hesitant to approach him."

Sasha shook her head in wonder. "I swear, if I didn't work for Westin and love what I do…"

"Yeah," Ryan said fervently. "Anyway, she'll let him know I'll be calling him when I get there."

"We."

"What?"

"We'll be calling when we get there."

He blinked. "I didn't expect you to go that far."

"I've gone further on a case."

"But this isn't a case for you, not really. Can you just leave?"

She picked up the folder she'd set on the floor. "Zach may have left Redstone to run the foundation, but he brought the philosophy with him. In fact, I'm willing to bet he'll offer any help he can."

Then she made her own call, to Zach's office at Westin.

"Sasha, there you are. We were wondering. Everything okay?"

"I'm with Ryan Barton," she said.

The pause was barely a split second before Zach said, "His sister?"

Reeve, Sasha guessed. Redstone apparently also had a grapevine that was unmatched. "Yes."

"Any progress?"

"Some. We think she went to Seattle to meet up with some guy she met online."

"Legit?"

"Don't know yet."

"So you're heading up there?"

She smiled at the assumption that proved her right; you could take the man out of Redstone, but not Redstone out of the man.

"Yes. As soon as we can organize it, I suspect."

"Hang on a sec." She heard him relaying what she'd told him to someone else in the room. "Reeve wants to know if you want her to go with you."

Sasha's smile widened. When you worked with people like this, maybe there was good reason to socialize mostly with them.

"Tell her thank you, but because we've only got some vague locations to go on, we need a local. Ryan's already got the name of somebody from Redstone up there. Security as well, in fact."

He relayed that information, too, and then there was a moment of rustling before Sasha heard Reeve's voice.

"Who?" she asked.

Sasha glanced at the name Ryan had typed. "Rand Singleton."

"Good," Reeve said. "He's a good man, one of the best. And his wife, Kate, grew up up there. Definitely a local."

"Good," Sasha echoed, then added, "If he's anything like you, I'm sure he is the best."

Reeve laughed. Sasha was glad to hear it; Reeve and Zach had gone through unimaginable hell, and it was good to hear her laugh so easily.

"What he is," Reeve said, "is pretty. Very, very pretty."

Sasha laughed in turn. "I can't wait."

"But then, Ryan is very, very cute."

Sasha's laugh faded, even though Reeve's tone was just as teasing. "Yes. Yes, he is. Still."

She was just hanging up, already working on shoving aside silly, unwanted emotions, when Ryan's cell rang. She waited while he answered, saw his expression change as he first listened, then uttered a fervent thank-you.

When he again closed his phone, she lifted a brow at him.

"We're going to Seattle."

"Well, yes."

"I mean, now. As soon as we can get to the county airport." He was on his feet then, going over to a secondary desk on the opposite wall.

"We have a flight already?" she asked, puzzled.

"Sort of." He looked over his shoulder and grinned at her. "On Redstone Air, I guess. There'll be a Hawk—not sure which one—ready and waiting in forty-five minutes."

She blinked. "We're flying on a Redstone jet?"

"We are."

He looked at the desk in front of him, and she realized he was contemplating the three laptops that sat there.

"Better take the best," he said, almost to himself. "Might have to do some more poking."

A little taken aback at how fast this was suddenly happening, Sasha focused on his words.

"Your 'best' laptop?"

He turned on her then, sounding defensive. "Would you think it was funny if a carpenter wanted his best hammer? Or a painter his best brushes?"

"Of course not," she said.

"You said they're tools. Well, these are mine, just as much as that hammer or brush is someone else's."

"I didn't mean it as a dig, Ryan," she said. "It's just…most people only have one. But it is your work, and I should have thought about that before I spoke."

He seemed startled, and she wondered just how much heat he'd taken over the years. He so didn't look like the stereotype of a computer geek, with his short, spiked hair, and his athletic build, but she supposed to some people nothing mattered beyond his fascination with the machines. That automatically put him in the geek category, with all its sometimes unflattering parameters.

"Do you suppose some people get weird about computer experts because they resent needing them?" she wondered aloud. "Or because the whole technology scares them?"

Ryan's mouth quirked slightly. "Yes," he answered.

She laughed, and so did he, so she guessed he wasn't holding her thoughtless remark against her.

While he packed up the laptop and some other gear, then threw some items in a duffel bag, she made a call to her parents to let them know she'd be out of town on a case. She got their answering machine, which was a relief; her mother still got nervous. Her work wasn't particularly dangerous, as a rule, since she did mostly the brain work, as Bedford called it, but her mother still worried.

She called Zach again, only to find they already knew she'd be leaving.

"Reeve was on the phone to Redstone the minute you hung up," he told her, "to be sure you had everything you need."

"Thank her," she said.

"I will. You need any reinforcements? Something just came in, but we can spare a body if you need someone."

"I don't think so. Not yet, anyway."

"Reeve says this guy Singleton's one of the best. She already called him personally, and he'll be waiting for you when you land."

"Wow. Redstone moves fast."

"Yes. Nobody pulls together for one of their own like they do."

By the time she ended the call, Ryan was ready to go. Men, she thought wryly. All they had to do was toss in some clothes, a razor, a toothbrush, and in Ryan's case probably not even a comb, and they were done.

Rather than juggle two cars, they took his, shifting them around so hers could stay in his garage. His was technically registered to Redstone, and it seemed better to have it sitting at the Redstone hangar at the airport. She wondered at the last glance he gave her little coupe as the door came down, but then they were in his blue Cruiser and on their way.

"Same place?" he asked.

She nodded, looking at the condo complex and thinking how far he'd come in that way, while she still languished in her rented apartment.

She had wondered if he even remembered where she lived, but when he made the first few turns without any direction from her it was clear he did. She tried not to read anything into that. He had a good memory, after all.

And then they were pulling up in front of her building. "I'll only be a few minutes. Do you want to come in?"

He seemed to hesitate. She wasn't surprised; she'd actually prefer it if he didn't. After all, her living room was the place where the physical attraction between them had nearly exploded, where they'd wound up half-naked on her sofa, and stopped only when Sasha had realized she was about to take an irrevocable step with a man she barely knew.

The memory was still vivid in her mind. It had taken her weeks not to think about it every time she walked through the room. She'd almost moved because of it. Especially when she realized she'd known on some level, even then, that it wasn't really going to work between them.

"I'll wait here," he said at last, and she hoped he didn't notice her relieved breath.

She'd always been comfortable in her apartment; it was spacious enough, with a large bedroom and a den that served as an office and could be converted to a guest room with the futon in the corner. But now, after the beautiful airiness and space of his condo, it seemed a bit dark and tired.

"So you spend all that time ragging on him about the future," she muttered to herself as she grabbed a small, rolling suitcase and started putting things into it, "and never really handle your own. Nice, Tereschenko, real nice."

But she would fix that, she vowed. As soon as they found Trish, she would start planning her own future.

She went for the basics in what she put in the bag. She wasn't sure what the weather up north would be this time of year, except likely cooler than here, so she went with layers built on basic black, with splashes of her favorite yellow in a sweater and a couple of blouses. And thought again of the touches of yellow in Ryan's home.

She headed for the bathroom and grabbed the things she used every day, figuring she could pick up anything she'd forgotten; it wasn't like they were heading into the wilds of Alaska. She took a moment to dig out a folding, travel hair dryer she'd bought and only used a couple of times; it went into one corner of the toiletries bag, which then went into the spot she'd left in the suitcase.

When she was done, she glanced at her watch: twelve minutes. Not bad. She hurried back outside. When Ryan saw her coming he got out and opened the back door of the Cruiser, and she tossed her bag in.

"Mail," she said suddenly, when they were rolling again.

"If it looks like we'll be there a while, we can put in a hold online," he said.

"Oh." She had thought she'd just call, hadn't even realized you could do that now. To each their own tools, she thought.

She'd never been to this back area of the busy county airport before, she thought as Ryan pulled up to a security gate a couple of blocks away from the entrance to the main terminal. He and the guard exchanged a few words before they were passed through, and Ryan turned left to drive along several rows of private hangars. They drove past a gap, a larger space between buildings, then slowed at a larger, longer building that stood alone at the end of the row, near the end of the airfield.

Unlike the other hangars, many of which had signs indicating their purpose or company name, this one was unmarked, the only clue to its ownership the red and slate-gray paint job.

Sasha heard the sound of a jet engine suddenly firing up. She looked, and saw a plane sitting near the end of the hangar. The matching color scheme told her this was a Redstone jet, and she guessed it was firing up for them. She felt an odd little thrill, and wondered at herself; planes were simply a method to get somewhere fast, she'd never been particularly fascinated by them. But this little jet was lovely, sleek and graceful. If even she, who didn't much care, could react like this....

I should have known, she thought. *You don't build an empire like Redstone if you don't start with something special.*

A young man wearing gray coveralls with a logo that looked like that very plane waved them into a parking area outside the office.

"Mr. Barton?"

Ryan nodded. The man in the coveralls was really little more than a boy, Sasha realized. He looked maybe nineteen at the most.

"I'm Tim. If you want to leave the key, I'll move the car inside when I close up," he said.

"Thanks," Ryan said, sliding the Cruiser's key off the ring and handing it over.

"We already gassed her up, and the gate called when you came through so she's fired up. You should be ready for takeoff shortly." An oddly gleeful grin crossed the young man's face. "Your pilot's raring to go, even though he just got back from an angel flight."

Sasha wondered what the amusement was about as they walked toward the plane. And what an angel flight was. Then she lost the thought as they went up the lowered steps into the little jet. She was surprised at how excited she was. Once inside, she barely had time to notice that the beauty of the interior matched the exterior before she heard Ryan mutter a heartfelt "Damn."

She turned, startled. Saw where he was looking, toward the cockpit, where a tall, lean man dressed casually in jeans frayed at the hems, a denim shirt and battered cowboy boots, was coming out.

"Didn't expect you," Ryan said, clearly stunned.

"But you're stuck with me," the man drawled lazily.

It hit her then. The boy's grin, Ryan's shock, the gray eyes and the drawl....

Their pilot was Josh Redstone himself.

Chapter 12

Once she got over the shock, Sasha was fascinated. She'd never met a bazillionaire before. Especially one who dressed like a cowboy just off the ranch. Which, she recalled from an article she'd read, he'd once been.

"I can't believe you're flying us yourself," she said.

"Happens I was the one free at the moment. And it gives me a chance to fly, which I never pass up."

Sasha doubted the head of one of the world's biggest organizations was ever truly "free," but it fit with what she'd heard of him, from Ryan, Zach and Reeve especially.

"It's still amazing."

He shook his head. "Ryan is Redstone. One of us needs help, we're all on call."

And that, Sasha thought, summed up what Reeve said was the Redstone philosophy quite neatly.

"I've never been on a plane like this before. It's beautiful, inside and out. And I generally don't even notice them," she admitted, then wished she hadn't; she didn't want to offend the man.

Josh—he'd insisted the formal Mr. Redstone she'd begun with wasn't for him—only laughed.

"But you noticed this one. Means I did my job."

She laughed in turn, relaxing a little. Behind him, she could see through into the cockpit, where there was a frightening array of complex-looking instruments.

"Want to sit up front for takeoff?"

To her surprise, her excitement rose at the idea. She glanced back over her shoulder where Ryan was already seated in one of the gray leather chairs, with his best laptop open in front of him on a table of some intricately grained light-colored wood polished to a high gloss.

"He's set for the duration," Josh said with a grin that lit up his gray eyes. Sasha couldn't help but smile back at him; it was infectious.

She followed him into the cockpit, shaking her head at the electronics jammed into the compact space. She was surprised Ryan wasn't up here regardless of how many times he'd flown on one of these. It was a measure of that intensity about finding his sister, she guessed.

"I gather you get Internet on board?"

Josh nodded. "Pretty solid, too. Ian Gamble invented a new kind of tracking satellite dish, and Ryan wrote the software for it."

She settled into what she assumed would be the copilot's seat. Josh seemed perfectly able to talk while getting ready for takeoff, and she was reminded that despite his relatively young age, the man had been flying for over twenty-five years. She would love to hear about that, what it had been like to learn to fly as a teenager, and how he'd taken his design for a small, fast, efficient jet and built it into an empire that spanned the globe.

Anyone not asleep knew that empire included not just a full line of jets but resorts to fly them to, along with countless other things that came out of their Research and Development

Division. Many were born of the fertile imagination of the man she knew Ryan admired most next to Josh, resident genius Ian Gamble. From a new insulin pump to prosthetic feet and legs, they were things that had changed the lives of thousands.

When she said as much, Josh glanced at her and smiled. "Ian is one of a kind." Then, almost as an afterthought, he added, "And he and Ryan make a hell of a team."

Sasha blinked. "Team?"

"Ian does the mechanics. Ryan does the programming that makes the mechanics work. Ian used to do both, but he's twice as productive now with Ryan. And happier."

There was a pause in the conversation as Josh spoke to someone, she assumed the control tower, on the plane's radio. Then the pitch of the engines changed, his hands moved easily over the controls, and they were rolling. When they eased into line behind a smaller plane behind a large airliner, she felt it safe to speak again.

"I didn't realize they worked so closely together, Ryan and Mr. Gamble. I know he thinks he's a genius."

"Ryan's a little in awe of Ian. We all are," Josh admitted. "His mind works in ways that are…well, unique. But it was Ryan who programmed the chip that makes that prosthetic foot you mentioned work so well. And the insulin pump. And right now, Ian's working on an idea Ryan came up with, to utilize a modification to the computer chip that powers some of our prosthetics."

Sasha shook her head. "I had no idea. I mean, I knew he'd written our search software, but—"

"And your facial recognition software, and that aging software."

Sasha blinked. "He did those?"

They used the facial recognition program a lot, and the aging software, as they called it, was one of their most useful tools. There were many variations of the program that could take a photograph of a child, and using other photos of older family members, project what that child would look like five, ten, even twenty years later. But theirs did something else useful that was rarer; it went the other way. And twice since she'd been at Westin, that capability had resolved cases so cold they'd been forgotten by all but the parents who lived every day with their endless grief. Once it had been a sad sort of closure, helping confirm a John Doe body was a long missing son, but once it had been a joyous occasion, with a girl kidnapped at age six reunited with her mother at age twenty.

She'd had no idea Ryan had done that. Or the other things Josh told her about. In all the time they'd spent together—which had been a lot in the three short months of their relationship—he'd never told her. He had to know it would impress her—anything that made her job easier did—but he'd never used it to win favor with her.

"Ryan's a special guy," Josh said. "He's taken a talent that got him into trouble and turned it into a solid and incredibly useful career."

"With help from you," Sasha said.

Josh shrugged. "I knew all he needed was a chance, a direction. And he's more than paid me back, countless times over, for any slight risk I took."

The words warmed her, although why praise for Ryan Barton would make her feel like this was something she didn't want to delve into just now.

"Like someone once took a risk for you?" she said instead. "Mac McClaren, for instance?"

"Heard about that, did you?"

"Ryan told me. I guess he's a treasure hunter in more ways than one."

She had the pleasure of seeing Josh Redstone smile almost embarrassedly.

"I'd say you paid him back, as well."

"Well, he can hunt to his heart's content and not worry if he finds anything. But," Josh added, looking oddly wistful, "he's found the biggest treasure of all in Emma."

There was something in that expression that made her heart

ache for this man she'd only just met. And since she had no idea what to say that wouldn't sound presumptuous—this was still Josh Redstone, one of the richest men in the world, after all—she kept quiet, except to let out an excited exclamation as the little jet took off and climbed at an angle that pushed her back into her seat. She found herself grinning, and when Josh glanced at her, he was grinning back, the wistfulness gone, and his love of what he was doing clear on his face.

They leveled off—at a much higher altitude than commercial jets had to stick to, Josh told her—and for a while she simply enjoyed the novelty and the view. Eventually she excused herself to go back and see what Ryan was doing. She took with her a confirmed opinion of one man, and a newly raised one of the other.

And the knowledge that Ryan Barton was no longer the heedless young man she'd once thought him.

If he ever had been.

Ryan looked up from the search results he'd been going through when Sasha came out of the cockpit and back into the cabin of the plane. She had the awed grin people often wore after their first flight on a Hawk; he'd be wearing it himself, despite the fact that he'd often been aboard before, were it not for Trish.

"Pretty slick, huh?"

"Yes," she said. "I still can't believe the man himself is flying us."

"That's Josh. And he meant it about never passing up a chance to fly. He doesn't get to nearly as much as he'd like anymore. He's always got work to do, so Tess usually flies when he's got to go anywhere on business."

"Tess?"

"His personal choice of pilot. She's amazing. She flew us on that search for Gabe's wife, and she was like a surgeon with a scalpel with that helicopter."

Sasha seemed to absorb that, and from her expression Ryan guessed that she liked the idea that Josh's chosen pilot was a woman.

She slid into the seat across the table from him. The bright yellow of her crisp blouse was a cheerful contrast to the richly elegant slate and red of the cabin. Just as it was in his condo.

Just as it was in his garage, he thought as the image came back to him. He liked the idea of her car tucked away in his garage. He was sure that meant he was heading down a slippery slope again, but there it was.

"What's an angel flight? That guy said Josh had just gotten back from an angel flight."

"Yeah. He's been doing that for years. Any Redstone plane that's not in use is available. All it takes is a phone call, and they're on their way to pick up a sick kid who needs to be somewhere else."

Sasha blinked. "You mean, like for special treatment or surgery?"

Ryan nodded. "Or sometimes it's to fly family to see the kid, or…"

His voice trailed off. Sometimes, too often, the flight was for a final visit, or worse, for a funeral. But given Sasha's devotion to helping kids, he wasn't sure that was something she'd want to know.

"I can guess," she said softly, and the look in her eyes told him she had. "Your boss is an amazing man."

"Yes. Yes, he is. The luckiest day of my life was the day I picked Redstone as a target."

And the unluckiest was the day you walked out of it, he thought, then grimaced inwardly. Ordering himself to knock off the stupidity—a tall order where she was concerned, it seemed—he went back to his search results.

"Still trying to get deeper into the network's records?"

"I'm there," he said, focused on the screen. "I just ran a search for any other screen names that come through that same Washington ISP, now I'm looking for any similarities between them."

"That's a great idea," Sasha said, sincere enough that it pleased him, surprised enough that it irked him a little.

"It happens," he muttered, not looking away from his screen.

"I should have thought of that. I'm glad you did."

Mollified, whether that had been her intent or not, he said, "It's basic to me."

"But smart. There's a chance he's done this with other girls. And if he's smart, too, then he'd set up a separate identity for each, since it's so easy."

Ryan looked up at her then. "It is easy, but why smart?"

"Most girls don't like to compete for a guy—the occasional female poacher aside—so it would be easier for him to convince her she's the one if he isn't flirting with a hundred other girls online in a public forum."

"Makes sense," was all Ryan said, but he was wondering yet again if there was a jab in there aimed at him. She'd told him two years ago that she didn't like competing with a machine for his interest, that she needed a guy who lived in the real, not the virtual world.

And you got all chapped about it and that was the end, he thought. He hadn't even considered whether she might have a point, he'd just reacted, like a guy who'd heard the complaint far too often.

The fact that he had didn't change the result, that she'd walked out. And she—

The sudden blip on the screen as his search results came back interrupted his thoughts. He looked at the list of names, wished for a moment that he was at home with his dual screen system, but downsized the windows and went to work, calling up the social networking home page and starting to run each name.

When he was done, he had a sick feeling in the pit of his stomach.

"Ryan?"

"If this is right," he said, not looking at her, "this guy's got at least three girls hooked or headed there."

She got up and quickly walked around to look.

"All these," he said, flipping through the pages quickly, "are, as far as I can tell, the same guy. I backtracked, and when

I got down deep enough, all these were set up by the same computer."

"You are a genius," Sasha said, leaning in.

He barely had time to warm to the compliment before his breath caught in his throat as she brushed against him. He caught the faint scent of the perfume he remembered; it had smelled like his grandmother's roses, and she'd told him she wore it in honor of her own grandmother.

"If I'm right," he finally managed to say.

"I think you are. They all have the same feel, the same lures."

"Lures?"

She flipped the pages almost as quickly as he had, pointing as she went. "Lonely poet boy, misunderstood, you're the only one who gets me, never felt this way before, all the stuff teenage girls are weak in the knees for."

"Now you tell me."

She gave him a startled look, took in his wry smile. And then she laughed, patting him on the shoulder. "I'm glad you didn't know. You would have been far too dangerous to the girls."

For a guy who'd never felt better than awkward around the girls his own age, girls who seemed so much different from himself that at sixteen he'd thought them a different species— with claws—those words were balm.

"Look," she said suddenly, pointing. "You *are* right. That photo was on one of the other pages, too."

He looked. "The dogs," he said.

"Another sure way to a girl's heart," Sasha said.

"Why is that? I mean, I know it works, I know a guy who even borrowed a dog to help him meet girls, but why does it work?"

"Any guy who can love a dog can love us," Sasha said simply. "At least, I think that's the reasoning."

He was curious now. He'd laughed at his buddy, until he'd ended up with more action than he could handle. "You don't think it's true?"

"I think the first part is. It shows a guy is capable of caring. And they're a great icebreaker. It's the assumption that that will somehow always transfer directly to us that is the failing of teenagers. Or women who still think like them." She gave him a sideways look again. "That being said, and all other things being equal, I'd go for the guy with the dog every time."

"Well, fine," he said, feeling suddenly grumpy about it. "My mom's allergic, we could never have one. And I'm at work so much now, it wouldn't be fair to the dog."

"Ah, but you get points for knowing that," Sasha said. "And you—"

She stopped as the computer popped up another result window. "I was running another search in the background," he explained, "to see if that same computer had left tracks anywhere else, and apparently it's a server for a Web site of its own." He clicked on the link. "This might tell us something more about the guy, where he is, if…"

His voice trailed off as he stared at the screen.

"Damn," Sasha said under her breath.

Ryan couldn't speak.

That it was a porn site was bad enough.

That it offered, for a fee, photos of young girls in varying stages of bondage and torture, apparently being held by the same man, a beefy, ordinary-looking guy with an extraordinary gleam in his eyes, made Ryan feel queasy.

A quick glance told him none of the girls on the front page were Trish, but he still felt sick. And the disclaimer in tiny print at the bottom of the front page, that all the "models" were over eighteen and had "posed" voluntarily, didn't alleviate the nausea in the pit of his stomach.

"You're sure this is the same computer?" Sasha asked, her voice tense.

"All the numbers match. It's either the same, or he's better than I am."

"I doubt that. So it's the same."

He knew it was.

His baby sister was in very, very big trouble.

Chapter 13

Reeve had understated, Sasha thought. Rand Singleton wasn't just pretty, he was breathtaking.

She tried not to be blatant about it, but she couldn't help staring as he stopped in front of them. Over six feet, lean but muscular, with startlingly dark blue eyes and hair in a shade of platinum Sasha had only before seen in children. It fell forward nearly to his eyebrows, and she wondered if his wife felt the same urge she did to brush it back with her own fingers.

They had flown into a small local airport on the west side of Puget Sound, their target zone. Redstone had a facility there, to avoid flying a private plane into SeaTac, Josh had told them. And since Rand lived on this side, it was easier for him as well.

Now, Josh performed the introductions, and Sasha couldn't help but notice the easy relationship apparent between them all. Like family, she thought. The family everyone said Redstone was.

"How's Kate?" Josh asked.

The smile that curved Rand Singleton's mouth could have powered the runway lights along this entire airstrip, Sasha thought. And it warmed her with its spillover; this was a man truly in love with his wife. It was possible, it reminded her, just as seeing Reeve and Zach almost daily reminded her.

"She's great. Always."

Josh nodded. "Back to her. And tell her distribution is now aware of her genius, after that shipping plan she came up with."

Rand laughed. "She is nothing less," he said. "But then, she's Redstone."

"And I'm beginning to see," Sasha put in, "what a very, very good thing that is to be."

Josh's grin was a little lopsided, as if he himself were sometimes surprised by the depth of loyalty he inspired. Then he indicated Ryan and Sasha with a gesture. "Whatever they need," he said.

"Of course," Rand said, as if it were a given. "Can you stay?"

Josh shook his head with every evidence of true regret. "Don't I wish. But I've got a dinner at five. One of those hideously boring ad agency things."

Rand glanced at his watch, then looked at his boss with a knowing grin. "Five? You're going to have to haul…butt."

Josh's brows rose, and in a tone of surprise that was clearly put on, he said, "Am I?"

"Never fly fast when you can fly faster?" Ryan said, earning a laugh from his boss.

"It's a win-win for me," Josh admitted. "I get to fly fast, or I get to be late."

Rand laughed. Then, with a sheepish grin, he looked at his boss and said, "Well, if you have to leave, I guess I get to just tell you. Kate wanted you to be the first outside the family to know…we're going to add to the drain on the Redstone benefits."

It only took Josh a split second to get there. When he did, he lit up. "A baby? Rand, that's wonderful news. Congratulations."

Sasha and, belatedly, Ryan—who looked a bit discomfited—added to the chorus. Rand gave them that electric smile again.

"Kate was a little startled. She thought if we wanted a baby, at her age it would take intervention, but…"

The smile widened and he shrugged, stopping short of looking like a very smug male and instead looking only deliriously happy, Sasha thought.

"When? Is Kate all right?" Josh asked.

"It's early yet. We just passed the danger mark of three months. She has her moments, but she's so happy about it in general she gets through them pretty quickly."

"Losing her little girl like that, I'd be surprised if she didn't," Josh said. "Some things you never, ever get over."

Sasha heard the note of quiet, pained endurance under the words, and remembered suddenly hearing from Reeve that Josh's beloved wife had died some years ago, and that he'd never been seriously involved with anyone since, let alone remarried.

"Everyone around him at Redstone seems to be falling in love and getting married with amazing regularity," she'd said. "But Josh…"

A few minutes later, after watching the sleek Hawk IV lift off and head back south, Rand ushered them toward the small building that served as an airport terminal.

"I'm assuming you want to get started right away, so let's go over what you've got in here," he said, leading the way toward an office in the far corner of the terminal building.

He pulled open the glass door etched simply with the Redstone logo and let them precede him. A young man on a phone looked up as they came in, smiled and nodded at Rand. Then his gaze flicked to Sasha and, gratifyingly, his eyes widened. So did his smile.

In that same moment she felt Ryan's hand on her back, as if she needed his guidance to find her way to the single, private office in the back of the relatively small space.

Or as if he was making a statement to the young man on the phone, she thought suddenly. Staking a claim?

Get over *yourself,* she thought sternly. It was ridiculous the way she was seeing everything through that filter. She'd never had so much trouble staying on task before, and she wasn't happy that it was happening now. True, she'd never spent so much time with someone she'd broken up with before, but still, it just shouldn't be this…silly.

She shouldn't be this silly.

"I'm sorry about your little girl," Sasha said to Rand, aware she was reaching for something to say to get herself past this moment of idiocy, but meaning it, too.

"Emily wasn't mine. I never got the chance to know her. She died a few years before I met Kate."

"Oh." *That's what I get for being an idiot.*

"It's…brave of your wife to try again."

Sasha turned to stare at Ryan, stunned at the perception in his quiet words.

"It is," Rand agreed. "She is. Among the many other amazing things she is. Now," he went on briskly, "let's get on to your business. What do we have?"

At his request, they laid it out for him from the beginning; Sasha appreciated that he was willing to take the time, and that he wanted everything they had. He seemed as intent on this as they were, and she knew she was seeing the Redstone philosophy in action.

The only interruption was Rand asking for the current photo of Trish, which he took a copy of with his cell and sent it to a number along with a brief text. When they got to what Ryan had discovered on the plane, Rand's eyes narrowed. "Son of a… Okay, that puts this in a lot more than just a runaway category."

He seemed about to go on, but hesitated, with a glance at Ryan.

"Believe me, I get it," Ryan said grimly.

"Time," Sasha said, "is really critical now."

Rand nodded, shoving that silky hair back with his left hand, a simple gold band glinting on his ring finger. "Okay, do you have a list of references this guy has made?"

Sasha nodded and pulled out the pages she'd been working on on the flight. "Here are the things and places he mentioned on Trish's page. And these—" she set out another page "—are the ones he's mentioned on other pages, under other screen names."

Rand scanned the pages, nodding occasionally.

"You have copies of the pictures that purport to be him?" was all he asked, and when Sasha handed him the copies they'd made he lapsed back into silence and kept reading.

When his cell rang, Sasha sensed Ryan tense. The conversation was rapid-fire.

"Hey, Mel. Yeah, California girl. About then, yes." Then Rand listened for a moment. "Thanks."

He hung up, and looked at them. "Friend of Kate's she used to mentor. She works part-time at the airport now, while she's going to college. At the transportation desk." Rand grinned. "Handy, sometimes."

"She saw Trish?" Sasha asked.

He nodded. "Said she asked for the best way to get to the ferry. Remembered her because she was so excited, and seemed really new to traveling. And nervous."

"So we know she made it here," Sasha said.

"And that she was headed to this side," Rand said.

Finally, as if he could wait no longer, Ryan spoke. "There are about four places he mentioned on all the pages, and a couple he mentioned more than anything else on Trish's."

Rand looked up at him, nodding. "Good place to start."

"We should split up," Sasha suggested. "Cover more ground faster."

Rand hesitated for a moment, then nodded. "Just be careful. If this bondage Web site guy turns out to actually be the guy who brought Trish here, he could be dangerous. At the least unpredictable."

"Wait," Ryan said, sounding troubled, "if you think Sasha could be in danger—"

"I've run into his type before," Sasha said, cutting him off. "Besides, I think I'm too old for him."

Ryan opened his mouth, then shut it again, as if he'd decided there was no way to safely say anything to that.

"Wise man," Rand said, one corner of his mouth quirking.

Sasha couldn't deny the accuracy of that. And coupled with his startling observation about Rand's wife, she was going to have to face soon the fact that Ryan Barton hadn't just changed, he'd changed a great deal.

Where that left her, she wasn't at all sure.

Ryan slid behind the wheel, taking a moment to familiarize himself with the location of the controls. When they'd agreed on a division of tasks, Rand had suggested they take his Redstone SUV, which had a good GPS system, and he would have one of the office staff take him to pick up his wife's personal car, since he already knew his way around. Summer Harbor, the small town where they lived, was a few miles away, but it would be worth it to cover more ground faster.

"Just don't let it get stolen," Rand said with a crooked grin. "There's some stuff in there I'd really miss."

There had been no real discussion of who would drive. It seemed logical to Ryan that he would drive the Redstone vehicle, and she hadn't even questioned him when he got into the driver's seat.

"I'm sorry we're taking you away from your wife," Sasha said as she walked around to the passenger side.

Rand laughed as he removed a couple of items from a locker in the back of the gray Tahoe, a metal box and a zippered leather case. "One of the first ground rules Kate laid down was no hovering or fussing."

Sasha laughed. "My kind of woman," she said, pulling open the door. "But then, that's easy for me to say. I'm not pregnant."

Ryan sat there, determinedly not going down any path those words pointed to, as she got in. They said goodbye to Rand, reiterating the promise to touch base every couple of hours. Since he would likely get there faster and easier, knowing the territory, he was going to take the places mentioned on all the pages their quarry had posted on, under one name or another, while Ryan and Sasha checked the two he'd mentioned most on Trish's.

"He's a nice guy," Sasha said as they headed toward the airfield's back gate.

"Somehow I don't think that's a woman's first thought about him." He was proud of how amused he managed to sound. It surprised him when Sasha answered very seriously.

"Absolutely not. But if that ring on his finger didn't stop any other thoughts, the utter glow in his eyes when he speaks of his wife would. That's an invulnerable bastion, that is."

She sounded, he thought as he paused to listen to the GPS's verbal directions, almost wistful. "Is that what…women want?"

She gave him a sideways look. "I don't know. I only know what I want. And, I suspect, what your sister wanted that got her into this."

And just that neatly, she'd steered the conversation away from herself and back to the reason they were here in the first place.

Which is what I should have been thinking about, not getting lost in speculation about a woman who made her feelings crystal clear.

Already they were out among the tall, thick evergreens that made this part of the world famous. Down south, they'd still be amid glass-walled high-rises and block after block of traffic and cranky drivers. It was, he thought, a very different world. No wonder so many fled up here. Too bad some of them brought their nastier habits with them.

Of course, some who were already here likely had some nasty ones of their own. Which again brought him back to the task at hand.

"Tell me again why we're doing this? I mean, if this guy isn't this kid, what good will showing photos around do?"

"We're doing this because we don't know for sure it's not really just a kid, because it's a place to start, and the only one we really have at the moment. And because you never know."

He had no answer for all that logic, and since it all made sense he just went on. "But that Web site," he began, then stopped as his stomach started to churn again at the memory of the images.

"I know, Ryan," she said gently. "But we really don't know. It could be someone hijacked a kid's ID. Those types are always hiding, as well they should. It could be a relative who's using him as a front."

His stomach knotted tighter. "For that crap? Who'd use a kid to front for that?"

"You'd be surprised," she said, and this time she sounded nothing more than weary.

He glanced at her, saw the set of her face, the way she was staring unseeingly at the papers she held. And for the first time he truly felt the weight of what she did. He'd known it, in his head, ever since he'd met her, but now he felt it in his gut, and he marveled at the fortitude it had to take to face what she faced, to see what she saw, on a regular basis.

He didn't know if even the joyous conclusions could make up for the bad ones. Not when they were as bad as he knew they sometimes were.

After making a turn and getting directions to continue for several miles, Ryan seized the distraction-free moments.

"How long can you keep this up, Sasha?" he asked quietly. "How long can you deal with this kind of thing until it eats you alive?"

"I'm doing an important job," she said.

"Beyond important," he said. "But at what cost?"

"Nothing near the cost paid by the loved ones of someone who's never found."

"But what about you?"

"I can handle it. It's what I do."

"But how long?" he asked again.

She gave him a sideways look he caught out of the corner of his eye.

"As long as I can," she said simply. "As long as I see Zach

Westin, who's been through the worst possible end to a missing child case, show up every day determined to save someone else from going through what he went through."

"But now that he and Reeve are married…doesn't she want him to ease up?"

"Reeve only reinforces that determination," Sasha said. "She felt so guilty about not saving Zach's little boy that it almost destroyed her, and she'd be the last one on earth to ask him to stop."

Ryan pondered that for a moment, then muttered, "Complicated."

"Life is. Because people are."

"Yeah, I get that," he said, an edge creeping into his voice.

"What?" she asked, apparently reacting to the sharpness.

"Just getting tired of the jabs."

"Jabs?"

She sounded, he thought, utterly unaware. "I know what you think of me. You made it clear two years ago. I don't need the reminders."

"Whoa." Okay, now she sounded startled. Genuinely startled. "You mean jabs at *you*?"

"People are complicated. Don't drink the Redstone water. My 'best' laptop. Some jerk of a guy looking for no-strings sex. That I didn't keep tabs on Trish, or check her page regularly. That I take my folks for granted. You know what I mean."

She was silent for a long, tense moment. "I'll give you the Redstone water one," she finally said. "And the laptop. I was teasing you. But the rest…they weren't aimed specifically at you, Ryan. They're how I feel, and believe it or not, are not all about you."

His jaw tightened, and he bit back the retort that rose to his lips.

"Just like," she said, her tone suddenly quieter, and almost sheepish, "it's not all about me, no matter how my brain keeps trying to make it that way."

The admission startled him. He flicked a glance at her. Was

it possible she'd been going through the same thing? Thinking casual comments were instead aimed directly at her? Had their brief but intense relationship two years ago actually built this minefield?

He opened his mouth to speak but was interrupted by the GPS telling him they were approaching the turnoff they needed. He slowed, exited the highway, made the directed turn at the bottom of the ramp. Almost immediately they were in even thicker trees, towering over them and blocking any view of the surrounding terrain. Were it not for the occasional glimpse of a home or other building through gaps in the trees, you could easily think you were in an untouched forest.

"There," Sasha said, pointing to a road sign indicating the public park they were looking for a couple of miles ahead. Sad-Breeze's posts about the place waxed lyrical, speaking of writing poetry and thinking about life, and Sasha had been immediately suspicious.

"It's just the kind of thing a guy would do who wants to impress a girl with his 'deep sensitivity,'" she said, her tone clearly indicating she thought that kind of feeling beyond most teenage boys.

Remembering himself at that age, he wasn't sure he could deny she was right.

"My mother and father fell in love when they were sixteen." He didn't realize what a non sequitur that would sound like until the words were out. But Sasha seemed to get his point.

"I didn't say it doesn't happen, just that it's rare. Passions run high at that age, every roadblock is a catastrophe, and every upset the end of the world."

"They have no perspective," Ryan said. Sasha's head turned quickly, and again he felt the surprise in her glance. It was starting to annoy him that she was so surprised at him.

"Exactly. Nobody suffers like a teenager, at least in their own eyes. Just look at your sister's posts."

He couldn't deny that. He knew Trish's life had been relatively free of disappointments, let alone heartbreak; the worst thing that he could remember was her tears over not being able to get a cat or a dog. Yet her posts seemed...well, almost whiny.

"I used to gripe to my mom about having to pick up my room, and complain to my friends about how unreasonable it was for them to expect me home at ten on a school night," he said as he pulled into the parking area for the waterfront park that lay along the edge of what the map said was the Hood Canal, a long, hook-shaped finger of the sound. "But I never would have posted the stuff she did for the world."

"Nor would I," Sasha said. "I like a bit of privacy, still." She looked at him as he pulled the car into a parking slot. "What's your reason?"

"For not? Too much chance for you to be defined by one unguarded moment during a really bad mood, preserved forever in cyberspace."

Again her brows rose. Exasperated, Ryan shut off the engine and turned in his seat to look at her.

"I'm not a teenager, so I wish you'd quit being so surprised when I don't sound like one."

She had the grace to color slightly. "I'm sorry. It's just...that's not something you would have said two years ago."

"So a guy can't change in two whole years?"

"Apparently he can," Sasha said.

She was out of the car before he could answer, and by the time he caught up with her, walking toward the water, the moment was gone.

"It is beautiful," she said. "And the view of that bridge is spectacular."

"Yeah."

"Floating bridge," he said. "That part opens to let boats through."

"Speaking of boats, that's a launch ramp, I guess."

He nodded. "So now that we're here, what do we do? Doesn't look like there's anybody who works here."

"But there are a lot of people. We start asking, showing photos."

He let her take the lead. She was the pro, after all. And he enjoyed watching her work, noticed the way she got people's confidence quickly, almost easily. Something about her approach, her demeanor or the urgent sincerity she was able to project, got through to them.

Not, he thought a couple of hours later, that it did any good. They'd talked to everyone there, and to new arrivals, and there was no recognition of any of the photos. Ryan noticed Sasha didn't talk only to the younger people but also the older ones, including now, a man walking a large dog who, at a guess, had to be at least eighty. Both of them, the dog in dog years, anyway.

Ryan wandered down to the water's edge, watching the boats out on this summer day, distracting himself from his worry about Trish by wondering why all you ever heard about the weather up here was rain. He'd about decided that the locals kept days like this a secret to keep from being overrun when Sasha came up behind him.

"Let's go," she said. "Nothing more we can do here right now. If nothing turns up elsewhere, apparently there are some regulars who fish here early in the morning."

Ryan nodded as he unlocked the doors to the car. He hadn't thought about that, that they'd need a place to stay. He'd have to ask Rand about that. It was nearly time to check in with him anyway.

As he settled into the driver's seat he reached for his phone, but before he could dial, Sasha blasted him out of his thoughts.

"So, I know you're not a jerk, but are you still the guy looking for no-strings sex?"

Chapter 14

"What the...?" Ryan was literally gaping at her. Sasha couldn't blame him. She had no idea what had made her say it.

Or at least that's what she told herself.

"Sorry. That was inappropriate, given why we're here, unprofessional."

"Ya' think?" he asked wryly.

"It's just...why did you think that was aimed at you?"

For a moment, she didn't think he was going to answer. And she couldn't blame him for that, either. After all, they didn't have the kind of relationship that entitled her to an answer to a question like that. And when they had, she hadn't asked. She'd just gotten fed up and left.

He glanced at his phone, then dropped it back onto the console between them. She noticed on the display there was no signal for his service. It wasn't until they were back out on the main road that he finally did answer her unexpected, uncalled-for question.

"Maybe because it's what I told myself I wanted."

"Told yourself?"

"When I was telling myself your dumping me was for the best."

"I didn't dump you," she said. "I simply said it wasn't working for me."

"Not much different when you're the dumpee."

"Ryan—"

"So, did you find someone who could live up to your requirements?"

"You make me sound like I've got a checklist," she said, stung.

"Don't you? Oh, not a written one, but in your head?"

"Of course not," she said. "I know what things are important to me, but it's not a checklist."

"I'll bet they're prioritized, though. 'I can live with this but not this, and this has to be there but this not so much.'"

Sasha felt herself flush as he unwittingly hit upon nearly the very words she'd once used to explain to a girlfriend what she wanted in a man.

"Of course," she said. "Everyone does that. Are you saying you don't?"

"Sure," he said easily. Too easily, she thought, and her guard went up. "I look for all the usual stuff. Great body, pretty face, y'know, all the arm-candy stuff. Don't care much if she can talk well, or make sense when she does, as long as she gushes over me. And if her eyes are sexy enough, I don't care if she really sees anything, except me. Oh, and it would help if she'd gaze up at me adoringly most of the time."

By the time he was done Sasha was laughing out loud. She couldn't help herself. She'd forgotten, truly forgotten, what a wickedly sharp sense of humor he had. And how often he'd made her laugh.

She'd lived without laughter for too long. She hadn't realized until this moment that despite the seriousness of their task, she'd laughed more today than she had in a long time.

"Touché," she said, giving him his due. "Nicely done. I—"

She broke off as Ryan's cell rang; obviously they'd gotten within range of a tower.

"Rand," he said as he glanced at the display. He pulled a headset she hadn't seen before out of a shirt pocket and slipped it over his ear and pushed a button.

"Barton." He listened for a moment, then said, "We haven't either, although we may have to come back in the morning to check with some regulars." Again a pause, then, "I'll ask her. Yeah, we're headed there now."

When he disconnected, he glanced over at Sasha.

"He had as much luck as we did."

She shrugged. "It's early yet." She looked at her watch, then out and around. "And then again, it's not. It just seems that way. I've heard it stays light until late up here in the summer, but wow."

"Rand says we can stay with them tonight."

He said it baldly, without preamble, as if in a rush to get it out.

"Oh? I hope he asked his wife."

"He said his wife assumed as much, when he told her we were here and why." Then, in that explanation that seemed all-encompassing, he added, "She's Redstone, too."

"I look forward to meeting her," Sasha said. It was a generic response, but in this case it was also true; she wanted to meet the woman who could put that look on Rand Singleton's face.

Their second destination was a small combination coffee shop and café, tucked in the middle of a bland-looking strip mall, but that was, according to the posts SadBreeze made on Trish's page, a haven for local teens.

"If you aren't into hiking or kayaking or any of the other outdoor crap everybody does around here, it's the only place to go," he'd written. "Live music on Tuesdays, and the owners are actually almost cool."

This wasn't Tuesday, but that didn't seem to have slowed

things much; the place was bustling. If they were markedly busier on music nights, Sasha thought as they went in, the place must be packed.

She noted the small, almost makeshift bandstand in one corner of the long, narrow room. So did Ryan.

"Good equipment," he said. "Even a small soundboard."

She wasn't sure what that meant, but gathered it was a mark of a more professional operation than this looked. "Expensive?" she asked.

"Not cheap," he answered, "but at the lower end of those things."

She lifted a brow at him. "Do you know this just because it's electronic and you know all?"

She was careful to keep her tone merely curious, and he responded that way. "I used to play in a band, some. Before I realized my keyboard talents should be restricted to the ones with letters on them."

She laughed. He could really be quite charming, she thought. And he did have that great sense of humor.

And he was still the cutest thing walking, let's not forget that, she told herself wryly.

The owners were a couple barely older than Sasha and Ryan, and they ran the place by themselves, with just a staff of two baristas for the coffee menu and two cooks for the surprisingly varied menu of sandwiches, soups and breakfast staples. They opened, the sign in the doorway had said, at 6:00 a.m., to cater to the commuter crowd on their way to the ferry to head into Seattle.

Sasha ordered a latte, but Ryan passed in favor of dragging out the photos.

The man, wearing a T-shirt from a small town in Alaska and with sandy hair long in the back and already thinning noticeably in front, shook his head.

"Check with Sandy. She pays more attention to faces than I do," he said.

At the sound of her name the woman, a tiny, energetic-looking brunette, came over, her hair held up in a ponytail by a whimsical scrunchie adorned with a plastic killer whale. She looked at Trish's image and shook her head as her husband had.

"He looks vaguely familiar," she said, pointing to the picture they'd pulled from the Web page. "But I may have just seen him around if he hangs out at Point-No-Point."

Sasha blinked. "Point what?"

She laughed. "The lighthouse. Out in Hansville."

"Point...No-Point?"

"Yeah. Short version, old-time sailors, looking for the entrance to the sound from the strait, thought they'd found the point they'd heard of, but it was only a big sandbar."

"Point, oops, no point," Ryan said.

The woman grinned. "Exactly. It's a great place. Views of Mt. Baker and Mt. Rainier, not a lot of places right here where you can get both mountains so clear."

When they'd finished showing the photos, with the owner's permission, to the other patrons, and netted the same results, they went back to the car.

Ryan glanced at his watch, then at the sky, which was finally showing signs that evening might get here eventually. "She said it's not that far to that lighthouse."

"You want to go look?"

"I'm not sure what good it would do."

"That's how this works," Sasha said. "No stone unturned, and all that."

The lighthouse was a bit farther out than they'd expected, requiring a long roll down a main road, then a U-turn that doubled them back the way they'd come, but on the other side of the rise and right along the water. The road narrowed as it veered left, past a small, flat camping area and down to the point itself and its lovely, sandy beach. There were three cars already parked there, apparently attached to the fishermen—and one woman—busily about their task. Ryan pulled into an empty slot, and they got out.

The lighthouse itself was small, the keeper's quarters

slightly larger. It looked shuttered and quiet, despite the chairs on the front porch. Sasha suggested they head for the lighthouse first, and Ryan simply nodded and followed.

"It's beautiful here," she said as they went.

"Windy," Ryan noted. "Do you think maybe this is that 'special place' he kept mooning about?"

"Maybe," Sasha said. "It would impress me, a guy who said this was his favorite place."

He blinked. "It would?"

"More than a mall or the local skateboard park."

"Guys only hang at malls because girls do."

"And don't those girls know it. Sometimes that's the first taste of female power they get, when they realize the boys are doing something they hate just to be around them."

Ryan gave her a startled glance, then a grin. "Should you be giving up the secrets of the sisterhood to me like that?"

"I wouldn't," she said solemnly, "if I thought you'd misuse them."

The grin slowly faded, and she knew he'd gotten her intention; an acknowledgment that he indeed wasn't a careless, thoughtless kid anymore.

"Thanks," he finally said.

"Sorry for the late realization," she answered.

It was an awkward moment, and when an older woman came out, dressed in khaki pants and a shirt with a logo for the United States Lighthouse Society above a name tag that said "Marty," Sasha welcomed the interruption.

"I'm sorry, did you want to see the light? Official tours are only on weekends, but I'd be happy to—"

"No, thank you," Sasha said with a smile that ameliorated the interruption. "But it is a lovely spot."

"We like it. The society moved here from a high-rise in San Francisco, and I can't tell you how exciting it is to be headquartered at an actual light."

"It's quite romantic, isn't it?" Sasha asked.

"Oh, yes," the woman said. She gestured at the light keeper's house. "The other half of the duplex is available as a rental, if you two are interested."

Sasha managed not to blush, but it was a near thing. "Are you here regularly?" she asked.

"Almost every morning." She smiled. "My husband and I, we're quite passionate about preserving this bit of history."

Sasha got out the picture and showed it to the woman. "Do you know this boy?"

The woman slipped the reading glasses that were on a keeper around her neck up to her eyes. "No, I'm afraid not. Obviously the photo was taken right at the tip of the point, but I don't recognize him, no."

"We think he may be here regularly."

"It's possible he might come before or after my hours," the woman said. "Lots of folks do. To some it's restful, to some exciting, to some—" Sasha caught the glance at Ryan then "—romantic, as you said."

If Ryan caught the subtle suggestion in the woman's tone and look, he didn't react. But the romantic reference did make him bring out Trish's photo. "How about her?"

The woman looked. Looked again. And frowned.

"You're looking for this girl?"

He nodded. He leaned in slightly, and Sasha knew he hadn't missed the woman's sudden shift in demeanor. "My sister. Trish. She's been missing for a week."

The woman sucked in a breath. "Oh, no."

"What?" Ryan said urgently.

"I believe I saw her here. A few days ago."

"Was she alone?" Sasha asked.

"No," the woman said, glancing at the photo Sasha still held. "But she wasn't with that boy, either. She was with her father."

Ryan went very still.

"They were arguing," the woman went on. "So loudly the other people on the beach were all turning and looking. Did she run away after that?"

"What were they arguing about?" Ryan was fairly vibrating with the intensity of the question.

"I couldn't hear it all, and I didn't want to eavesdrop on a family affair, so I went back inside."

"What did he look like, this man?" Sasha asked.

The woman gave Ryan a curious glance. "But if she's your sister—"

"Please, Marty. What did he look like?"

The woman looked at them both, her troubled expression deepening. "Oh, dear. It wasn't her father, was it? I thought it was just the typical teenage girl arguing with a parent, but when he yanked her toward the car so hard I wondered—"

She stopped herself in the moment before Sasha sensed Ryan was going to explode, and quickly answered the question.

"He looked mid-fifties. A bit stocky. His hair was dark, but shaved short. He looked very angry. His eyes…"

Sasha didn't have to look at Ryan for his reaction.

The woman had just described perfectly the evil-eyed man in the photos on that hideous Web site.

Trish wasn't just in trouble, she was in danger.

Chapter 15

"There," Sasha said, pointing at the small, carved wooden sign that said Redstone Northwest.

Ryan nodded and pulled in, wondering where the heck the place was; this winding drive curved through trees that looked as if they'd been here forever, undisturbed. He was beyond antsy; ever since they'd talked to the woman at the lighthouse he'd been on the edge of panic. Sasha had asked more questions after Marty had told them about the man, but he'd been barely able to think.

Finally they reached a cluster of buildings, smaller than he'd expected, and each clad in identical wood siding and painted in the Redstone scheme of slate gray and red. The overall impression was more of a lodge than business, and certainly not a manufacturing business. He knew they produced Ian's revolutionary new insulin pumps here, and that the demand for them was massive, so he'd expected something more…massive. Leave it to Redstone to do the unexpected. But he had to admit the buildings blended with the surroundings, the trees masking the actual size of the complex, and with none of the individual buildings so huge they overpowered the site.

He spotted Rand leaning against a blue coupe, cell phone to his ear, and pulled to a halt beside him. As they got out of the Redstone vehicle, Rand held up a finger to indicate he'd be done in a moment. Then he snapped the phone closed.

"We should have a list of possible cars soon," he said. "St. John is nothing if not efficient."

Ryan nodded; the mysterious man seemed to work miracles.

"There seem to be a lot of those hybrids up here," Sasha said. "If Marty was right about that being the car he was driving, it could be hard to narrow down."

"But better than starting with every car in the county," Rand said. "And better than if they were on the other side, in Seattle."

"I'm surprised he isn't," Sasha said. "I'd think it would be easier to hide among more people."

"More privacy over here, maybe." Rand shrugged. "Whatever, we'll find him. And Trish," he said, shifting his gaze to Ryan.

"There has to be something we can do, now," Ryan said. "I can't just wait until morning, not when she's out there with this perv."

"There is," Sasha said. "We can think. Go over things again. We have a tiny bit more information that we didn't have before."

"That's not what I meant," Ryan muttered.

"I know. You want an enemy to confront. But we don't have that yet."

That was exactly what he wanted, but he hadn't expected her to understand that.

"Follow me back to the house," Rand said. "You're going to need food and rest before anything else. You won't do Trish any good if you're stumbling around exhausted and too hungry to focus."

Reluctantly, Ryan had to admit he was right. It had been a long and exhausting day. He pulled the driver's door open again, glancing back the way they'd come.

"That's quite a driveway," he said.

Rand nodded. "As usual, Josh wanted the least obtrusive complex they could build. It makes bringing bigger supply trucks in and out a challenge, but Josh's view is that if the driver can't do it, he shouldn't be driving for Redstone, and if he won't do it, he doesn't understand Redstone."

Sasha smiled, but Ryan merely nodded. Redstone wasn't one of the best places to work just because it paid well and the bennies were good. Josh expected, and got, the best from his people. His motto of "Hire the best and then get out of their way" had served him well for a long time now.

"Do you work from here?" Sasha asked.

"More from home," Rand said. "They have their own security guy, Brian Fisher. He's a little young yet, but he's coming on, and they don't need me. So I handle anything else that comes up here in the northwest, Redstone Canada, Alaska and most of our Pacific Rim stuff."

"Sounds exciting."

"Sometimes. But we prefer boring." He pulled open the driver's door on the blue coupe. "Follow me. We should make it before it's too dark to see."

It was a twenty-minute drive, but it seemed longer to Ryan. He told himself it was the lack of landmarks; he was used to a gas station on every corner and a strip mall or restaurant every three blocks. Here there were only trees, and more unsettling were the countless side roads with no signage at all, just posts with numbers; if you belonged there, you knew, he guessed.

But in fact, he knew it was worry that made time drag. And even knowing Rand was right, and there was little more they could do tonight as it neared nine o'clock, didn't ease the feeling.

The town of Summer Harbor, population 2735 according to the sign they passed, was, if nothing else, picturesque. Harbor might be a bit grandiose a title for the little inlet, but it had a small marina full of boats, so Ryan figured it qualified.

Sasha exclaimed with pleasure when they pulled up to a small house set amid tall trees, through which there was a glimpse of the blue water of the inlet. In spite of his anxiety Ryan smiled inwardly; of course she liked the house, it was yellow. A lighter shade than her own favorite, but still yellow. And cheerful, he had to admit. It must be like a spot of sunshine on a gray day, which was perhaps the reason for it up here in rain central.

She exclaimed again when they parked, grabbed their bags, and met Rand at the front steps; there was a two-person swing at one end of the covered porch that Sasha immediately pronounced charming.

"Seems to be the female reaction," Rand agreed.

"You don't like it?" Sasha asked, surprised.

"It has its moments," Rand said, his tone bland, but the corners of his mouth twitching. Ryan immediately knew what the other man was thinking; that swing, Ryan guessed, indeed had its moments. And suddenly he saw the attraction of all these trees and the privacy they provided.

"Kate was renting the place when we met. She loves it, so we bought it last year, and added on an extra bedroom and bigger office this spring." His mouth quirked upward. "We didn't realize her old office was going to end up a nursery, and we've got a lot of work to do to get it ready, but at least it's already here."

The door opened before they got there, and Ryan thought the smile of the woman standing there when she saw them was nearly as breath-stealing as Sasha's. It began when she looked at Rand, but grew to encompass them all as she ushered them inside. She didn't look pregnant, but Rand had said it was early yet. And Ryan quickly saw why Rand was so enraptured; the dark-haired Kate Singleton wasn't a turn-your-head-on-the-street beauty, but that smile lit up eyes that were an incredible shade of gold-green, and for that instant you couldn't look at anything else.

"I'm Kate, welcome. I wish it was under other circumstances. But it will be, soon," she said, covering all bases with an efficiency Ryan couldn't help but appreciate. Her apparent confidence that they'd find Trish didn't hurt, either.

"Thank you," Sasha said. "Especially for taking us in on such short notice."

"Ryan's Redstone," she said simply. "And you're close enough," she added to Sasha. "I've heard wonderful things about your foundation. And I met your boss once, when I visited Redstone Headquarters, when he still worked there."

"Zach? He's the best."

"I felt awful for him, about his little boy."

Something tugged at Ryan, some new awareness, born of his worry about his little sister. An image of her tugging at his hand and looking up at him adoringly when she'd been little more than a baby flashed through his mind.

"And you would know," he said quietly, gently. "It shouldn't happen to anyone."

"No," Rand said as he slipped an arm around his wife. "It shouldn't."

Ryan wasn't sure he could eat anything, but when Kate set out bowls of rich, thick clam chowder and crusty rolls, his stomach woke up.

"Sun's up early this time of year, so we'll get a good, early start," Rand said as they sat down at the table.

"Yeah," Ryan said, but he wasn't at all sure what that meant. Where to go, what to do.

But Sasha did. He glanced at her, where she sat to his right, and found her watching him. She wore an expression on her face he couldn't quite name, but somehow it warmed him.

Sasha woke up with a start, aware she was in an unfamiliar room in the instant before the world righted itself and things slid into place in her mind. The guest room was more than comfortable. It was welcoming, with its yellow and blue color scheme and the lovely, curved sleigh bed.

One room or two?

Kate's discreet question last night had made Sasha blush, something rare enough to merit some thought later. But she had been tired enough that she'd only gotten as far as wondering, before falling asleep, if Reeve had somehow mentioned something.

But now, this morning, she knew better. Reeve would never interfere like that.

Which meant, she thought as she went into the compact three-quarter bath that was attached to her room, there had to be another reason Kate had asked.

Maybe the fact that you were watching Ryan like a hungry cat last night?

She grimaced as she looked at her tousled hair and still-sleepy eyes in the mirror. Ryan, she knew, was in what had once been Kate's office and would soon be the baby's room, on a sofa bed Kate swore was actually comfortable.

He would have been more comfortable in here.

This time her grimace was at her own thoughts. She peeled off the silky sleep shirt—in her preferred yellow, of course—she'd brought and stepped into the shower.

And you both would have had more fun.

"Stop it!" she said out loud, and it echoed off the tiled shower walls. The house was equipped, Rand had told her, with Ian Gamble's version of a tankless water heater, so hot water wasn't an issue and she could shower for three hours if she wanted to.

There had been a glint of satisfaction in his blue eyes that had told her he had some experience with that, and she wondered if that was how Kate had wound up pregnant. A thought she could have done without, as images of the possibilities of this spacious shower shot through her mind.

And you could both use some fun right now.

Usually the little voice in her head was helpful. This morning it was simply irritating.

But she couldn't deny she'd been touched by Ryan's unexpected sensitivity to Kate's loss, and for that matter, Zach's as well. He hadn't known either of them when it happened, but he'd obviously made the connection and expressed a sympathy that was sincere but not cloying.

They had been up late, after Kate, pleading a new and unaccustomed need to sleep more, went to bed. They had gone over what they had accomplished that day, and reluctantly looked again at the disturbing Web site.

"How do people get so twisted?" Sasha whispered, wishing she didn't have to look.

"I don't care how he got that way, I just want his ass," Rand said grimly.

"I'm with you," Ryan said. "I don't care why a spider's a spider, not when he's messing with mine."

The words were fierce, the sentiment pure male. Protective. A bit primitive, perhaps, but when you were the one being protected....

Sasha had the oddest sense that she'd somehow hit a tipping point. It took her a moment to realize it was because in that moment, she was thinking of Ryan not as a boy any longer, but as every bit the man Rand Singleton was.

And since that was the main reason you had for leaving him....

"Shut up!"

She felt more than foolish, snapping at herself, and was thankful the running water masked the sound.

She hurried through the rest of an abbreviated routine, dressed quickly, and headed out to where she heard sounds in the homey, warm kitchen. Where, to her surprise, the delicious smell that hit her nose was the result of Rand himself presiding over a couple of skillets.

"He cooks?"

Rand looked up with a grin. "Good morning to you, too. And yes, he does."

"Lucky Kate."

"She gets to do the seafood. I can't seem to acquire that

knack. She says sorry to miss you this morning, but she had a meeting at Redstone."

Sasha glanced at Ryan, who was off to one side, buttering toast. Tension fairly radiated from him, and she guessed the idea of breakfast had been forced on him, that he'd much rather be on their way.

Rand seemed to sense it, too, because the moment they sat down to eat the savory omelets and hash brown potatoes, he spoke between bites.

"Sorry to discuss such things over good food, but we should plan the attack."

Ryan was instantly at attention.

"I've got the list of cars," Rand went on. "St. John already did the basics, eliminating those that were listed as wrecked or outside the radius we discussed. The ones listed as the right color are on top."

St. John, Sasha thought, was living up to his reputation. Frank, even with his police contacts, couldn't have done it any faster.

"What if it's been painted?" Ryan asked.

"We can't assume it hasn't been at some point," Sasha said, "but let's not start out there."

They'd agreed, given the photos used and that they were all apparently taken "on the rainy side," as Rand put it, to limit their search to Western Washington.

"I figure we should start with the closest in to the most common spots he mentioned or showed," Rand said, "and work our way outward."

Ryan nodded, as did Sasha.

"I isolated the best head shot of the guy I could find on the Web site, and printed out copies," Rand said. Then, with a grimace, "Should have thought of that at the airport office."

"We didn't know for sure he was involved, then," Sasha said. "We'll go back to the lighthouse, see if Marty recognizes him as the man Trish was with."

She said it briskly, businesslike, knowing it was going to hit Ryan like a punch. He didn't speak, but she saw his jaw tighten.

She pushed on, hoping that having a plan would help him get through this.

"We should probably go back to the café, too, and see if they recognize him. Marty might not be there this early anyway."

He only nodded, but finished eating in a rush and politely put his dishes in the dishwasher. She followed suit, taking a moment to thank Rand for the meal, for both of them.

With a glance at Ryan, Rand nodded in silent understanding.

When they were back in the car and on their way, he seemed to relax just slightly. But he stayed silent, and the frequent tapping of his fingers on the steering wheel betrayed his mood.

"Were you hoping we'd just get off the plane and find her?"

He gave her a sideways look. "Hoping? Yes. Expecting? No. I didn't think it would be that easy."

Glad of that, Sasha only nodded.

The café was bustling, having been open a couple of hours already. It took them a while to corner the couple trying to keep up with the orders. They spared a quick glance at the photo.

The man, in a Montana T-shirt today, shook his head. But Sandy, her hair down today, took one look and wrinkled her nose.

"Oh, yeah, I remember him. He used to come in a lot, afternoons. He hasn't been around in a while though. I'm glad. He gave me the creeps."

Sasha felt Ryan tense, but forestalled him with a touch on his arm. "Why's that?"

"He always showed up about the time the high school let out. We get a lot of kids in about then. What creeped me out was the way he watched them."

"Did he ever approach them?"

"Nah, just watched. But he always had this smile on his face that…" Her voice trailed off, indicating she couldn't describe what she meant.

"Do you remember when you last saw him?"

She shrugged. "Two, maybe three months."

"Boys or girls?" Ryan asked.

Sandy shifted her gaze to him, her brow furrowed. "What?"

"Did he watch boys or girls?"

"Oh. The girls." Sandy brushed back a lock of hair. "He seemed to like the quiet ones. The cheerleader types that everybody else was tracking didn't even seem to register with him."

Ryan said nothing as they left and headed toward the lighthouse on the chance that the dedicated Marty might be there early, but Sasha could sense his tension was even greater than before. From the beginning she had questioned the wisdom of Ryan being so closely involved, but she'd known better than to think she could get him to just let her handle it.

There was only one vehicle parked at the lighthouse when they arrived, and Sasha thought it had been there yesterday as well.

"Marty, I hope," she said as Ryan parked.

It was, and the woman recognized them immediately when they knocked on the door of the office that took up half of the duplex of the former light keeper's residence.

"Did you find your sister?" Ryan shook his head, and she looked genuinely concerned. "I've been trying to think, to remember anything else, and—"

She stopped when Ryan held out the new picture.

"Was this the man?"

She pulled up the reading glasses again. Looked at the photo. Then up at Ryan.

And said the words they'd dreaded.

"Yes. That's him."

Sasha didn't look at Ryan. Couldn't. She didn't want to see the knowledge in his eyes. Trish was in serious trouble.

She could only hope that he hadn't followed the thought to what she, sadly, knew was an entirely possible conclusion.

Sasha didn't know what this man did with the girls he used when he was done with them, but she knew enough about his type to know that none of the options were pretty.

Chapter 16

Ryan fought the nausea that threatened as images from that disturbing Web site flashed through his mind.

Trish, what have you done? What have you gotten yourself into?

"—see him again, would you call me, please?" Ryan tuned back in as Sasha handed Marty a card with her cell number on it. "Trish could be in danger. He's not a nice man."

"Oh, dear," Marty said. "Of course I will. What a horrible thing, when you can't even trust a teacher."

Ryan went still. "A teacher?"

"Well, maybe not, but a school person anyway."

"Marty, what makes you think he was connected to a school?" Sasha asked gently.

Ryan wondered how she could stay so calm and speak so quietly when he was about to leap out of his skin. But then, that could be part of what made her so good at what she did.

"That's what I was about to say, that I'd been trying to

remember. There was a parking decal in the window of his car. Madrona College."

"Is that a local school?" Ryan asked, trying to follow Sasha's lead and rein in his urgency.

"Yes and no. It's on this side, but about thirty miles north of here. It's a community college."

"So he could have been a student, adult classes or something?" Sasha asked.

"Except," Marty answered, "the decal said staff."

"Did you notice if it was current?"

Yeah, she was good, Ryan thought. He wouldn't have thought to ask that, even though it was obviously important to know. But he knew they were on the right track. It all fit, too perfectly. A community college, where kids right out of high school might go who weren't sure of what they wanted, or just to placate parents who wanted them to go, or who were simply afraid of life after school.

Easy prey, he thought.

"Afraid not," Marty said regretfully. "I only recognized it at all because my daughter went there for a couple of years."

Ryan was glad Sasha had the calm to thank the woman, because he was way past the niceties.

"We've got him," Sasha said, touching his arm. She did that, he'd noticed. And had wished the circumstances were different so that he could appreciate it more. "Or we will soon. All it's going to take is to cross-reference a list of school employees with the registered owners on those hybrid cars."

"And how do we get that list?"

"Call Rand," she said. "He's got the contacts up here. Or maybe your St. John can do this."

Ryan nodded. He was sure St. John could do damn near anything. He made the call.

"For once I wish we had a computer handy, with a mapping program."

"We do."

Sasha looked at Ryan, who shrugged. "It's in my backpack. I thought it might come in handy."

They were headed toward the school, awaiting Rand's call, hopefully with the information they needed. Rand had agreed with Sasha's opinion that they not approach anyone; they didn't want to spook this guy, not before they found Trish. That, she'd told Ryan, was another of the perks of being a private agency; the police had to worry about putting the bad guy away, whereas Westin's only concern was to find the missing person. If in the process the bad guy went down, all the better, but the victim's safety was the goal.

It was Ryan who'd had the idea to look at the registered owners' list they already had and see what vehicles were registered in the area around the college.

Moments later she had the laptop open and booted up, and began to plot the addresses from the list. She glanced up when Ryan pushed a button on the in-dash GPS.

"Mute," he explained. "So it won't distract you."

"Thanks," she said, although she was quite capable of tuning such things out when she was focused. Of course, this case hadn't been her most shining hour for focus. But now that they were following a real lead, she'd do better, she knew.

"Geez, do these people drive anything else?" she muttered after a while as she entered another address that added yet another pin to the already studded map.

"We're about halfway there. What's the closest address to the highway?"

"If we stick to the ten-mile radius we discussed—" she looked at the map, found the highway, and clicked on the closest pin "—it's this one. Looks like it's about four miles ahead, fairly close. You want to go by?"

"I don't know. Maybe we should just keep going to the school, see if the car's there."

"We could—"

The ring of her cell cut off her thoughts; they'd told Rand to call her back, since Ryan would be driving.

"There are three exact matches," Rand said, dispensing with formalities.

Sasha grabbed the printout. "Go ahead."

"Page two. Chris or Rick Myers. About halfway down."

She ran a finger down the column, found the name, check marked it.

"Same page. Dennis Carlton, near the bottom."

She did the same with that name.

"Ron Nichols, top of fourth page."

She repeated the process. "These are the silver ones?"

"Yes. There are four others, I'll give you those, too, just in case."

She marked those names with a dash as he read them off.

"Where are you?" Rand asked.

"Nearly to the school. But I'm thinking we should check the addresses first, now that we have them, while these people are most likely at work."

"I agree," Rand said. "I'm going to head that way."

Sasha sensed something in his tone. She'd heard a great deal about Redstone Security, first from Zach and later from Reeve. She knew what it took to build a reputation like theirs, around the world.

She also knew she'd be a fool to ignore the instincts of one of their best, as Reeve had said Rand was. And so her next words were not really a question.

"You think this is the right track, don't you?"

"My gut does," Rand said. "I'm about forty-five minutes out, over on the island. I'll call you when I'm close."

"All right."

"Sasha?"

"Yes?"

"Keep him out of trouble, if you can. He's on a razor edge right now."

"I know."

"If it were my sister," Rand began, then trailed off.

"I understand," Sasha said.

When she'd closed her phone, Ryan glanced over at her. "He thinks we're right?"

Sasha nodded. "He said his gut does."

"That's good enough for me. Redstone Security didn't become legendary for nothing."

As soon as they passed a road sign that told her where they were, Sasha went back to the map program, finding the pins for the three addresses. Selecting the closest one, she gave Ryan directions.

"Not quite the GPS," she said, trying to lighten his mood, ease some of the tension she could feel building in him.

"But easier to listen to."

Surprised, she flicked a glance at him. He must have seen it out of the corner of his eye because he lifted his right shoulder in that half shrug she'd come to know.

"I like your voice. I always did."

It was a different enough compliment that it made her smile. "Thank you."

"I liked everything about you," he said, and suddenly they were in much deeper waters. "I admired what you do, your dedication, your drive, your energy, the way you can talk to people, empathize with them."

She was staring at him now. All he'd ever said when they were together was the typical surface stuff about her looks, her smile, her laugh.

"Why didn't you ever say so?"

"It sounded…too phony to me, then. Like a line, trying to impress you."

"Then why say it now?"

"Because I've always wondered if you would have stayed if I had said it then. Because I finally figured out that those are things that mean more to you than 'You look great.'" The half shrug came again. "Because it's true."

Oh, yes, very deep waters.

But where they had once been too cool for her liking, they

now seemed warm and welcoming, and Sasha realized with a little jolt she was seriously considering jumping right back in.

The first address was an ordinary house tucked into a stand of tall evergreens, somewhat reminiscent of Rand and Kate's home. The silver hybrid from their list sat in the driveway.

And a man in a wheelchair, his left leg in a cast and propped up on a leg rest, sat on the front porch.

Ryan was a bit taken aback when Sasha told him to stop, and more so when she hopped out and walked up to the man, who watched her with equal amounts of curiosity and appreciation. The first made him wary, the second, simply irritated.

He could hear the conversation as Sasha easily obtained the information, after asking for directions to the nearest gas station, that the man had broken his leg skiing three weeks ago, and that he was about to go stir-crazy, and his wife was ready to break his other leg.

When she got back in the car, his first question was, "Do you believe him?"

She nodded. "There were a bunch of signatures on his case. A couple of them mentioned the date, and they were all at least two weeks ago."

"So he's out."

She nodded. She didn't seem bothered by it, and he guessed she was accustomed to useless exercises.

"Process of elimination," she said, as if he'd spoken his thought. "It's the biggest part of the job."

He knew she was right, but it didn't make it any easier to rein in his urgency.

Trish, he thought, fighting the ache that rose in him. His little sister was out there somewhere, possibly—probably, he made himself admit—in a very bad kind of trouble.

"We'll find her, Ryan. I promise you."

Ryan nodded. He knew she meant it. They would find Trish. He just didn't know if they'd find her in time.

* * *

The second house was also a fairly ordinary-looking, wood-sided two-story, set on a large cleared lot amidst a grove of big trees that made the setting seem secluded. But this house was made rather spectacular by an intricate, perfectly maintained formal garden. There was a gravel path that ran arrow-straight from the street to the front door, not even a sprig of green daring to poke through and mar the groomed surface. On each side was a matching semi-circle of plantings, in matching order, and bordered by matching curved hedges that, Sasha suspected, would be exactly the same height and width if measured.

"Someone's got way too much time or money," Ryan muttered.

"I would have thought the symmetry would have appealed to you."

"Exactness is necessary for computers," he said. "In real life, it's a bit…"

"Boring? Oppressive? Anal-retentive?"

"All of those," Ryan said, managing a slight smile.

He got out as she did, but hung back as they'd discussed; she was simply less likely to set off alarm bells and send their guy running. And since he had no way of knowing who she really was or what she was after, Sasha insisted she was safe enough. But Ryan still got out of the car, and he'd be watching like the eagle they'd spotted on the way here.

"What are you going to say this time? I mean, the directions were a good ploy with the guy already outside, but knocking on the door?"

"Why, I'll say I just had to stop and compliment them on their lovely garden."

He'd been right, he thought as he watched her walk casually down that perfect path to the front door. If you could design a computer to work the way her mind did, you'd definitely have something amazing.

No one answered the door. She walked to one side of the

house, toward the equally pristine gravel driveway, and headed toward the back of the house. Ryan moved then; he didn't want her out of sight. He caught up with her near the garage at the end of the drive. There was a large combination shed and greenhouse next to it, both empty of anything but gardening supplies and plants.

"Whoever it is, they're beyond a hobby. This is a lifestyle," Sasha said as they walked back to the car. "And not a bad one to have, I guess. Those flowers are gorgeous."

"I always thought my mom was a gardener, but this is another level altogether."

"Frankly, I like your mother's garden better. It's…friendlier."

He was surprised at how the appellation fit, but knew she was right. His mother's garden was a slightly out-of-control profusion of whatever she liked, and as a result welcomed rather than impressed.

He was even more surprised at his own thoughts; he'd never analyzed such things before, just accepted what was and went on.

He still, it seemed, had things to learn from Sasha Tereschenko.

The third address had his radar humming the moment they found the battered mailbox with the street number. The same tall evergreens were thick, but here surrounded the house. Beneath the trees grew countless graceful ferns that looked like the kind his mother nursed and babied year-round in Southern California, but that apparently grew wild here, lush and tall and very unlike their spindly-by-comparison cousins to the south.

But what really got his attention was the padlocked, heavy metal gate across the driveway with the bold, stern "Keep out." There didn't seem to be any fence, however, the concern seemed mainly to keep vehicles out.

"Well, now," Sasha said. "That's interesting."

When she looked at him, Ryan saw an odd gleam in her dark eyes. And he realized suddenly he was seeing another side of her. This was the woman who had dedicated her life to finding missing children, the woman who attacked the job with fierce determination.

This was the woman who wasn't going to let a little thing like a locked gate interfere with that job.

Even as he thought it, she gave him a smile that seemed equal parts resolute and reckless.

"Wanna go for a walk in the woods?"

He couldn't have said no to those words in that voice under any circumstances. Under these, he was out of the car even before she was.

It wasn't easy walking, the undergrowth was so thick. And when they spotted the first building, the radar's hum increased; the house was ramshackle, run-down and painted in various patches of color as if they'd used whatever they had or could find thrown in a Dumpster somewhere. Its roof was literally green with thick moss.

There were also at least two outbuildings he could see, one that looked like a newer, small barn, and one a smaller shed-like structure with a moss-encrusted shingle roof that echoed the one on the house. Next to that was parked the car that had led them here.

And around it all was a shiny new chain-link fence.

He was startled out of his concentration on the layout when Sasha took his hand. For an instant, feeling her fingers curve around his, he forgot to breathe.

"We're just a couple out for a romantic ramble in the woods," she whispered. "Too stupid to realize we're trespassing."

He was annoyed at himself when her words calmed his suddenly racing pulse. Not that it slowed, but that it had sped up to begin with.

They worked their way closer, but stopped at the trumpeting bark of a very cranky-sounding dog. They froze as a man suddenly appeared in the doorway of the building.

It wasn't the man in the photo. But that didn't matter at the moment.

What mattered was the rifle in his hands.

Chapter 17

Ryan's heart was hammering as they crouched down, now grateful for the thick undergrowth. He was also happy for that brand-new-looking fence. But somehow he had the feeling it wasn't just to keep the large dog—some blend that resulted in a massive chest and head and a lean, muscular body—contained.

The dog's nose was pointed right at them. A few minutes spun out as they barely dared breathe. The dog clearly knew they were there, but as is typical with some people, the armed man trusted his own much weaker senses; when he saw and heard nothing, he snapped at the dog and walked back inside.

Ryan heard Sasha let out a long breath. "That was close," she whispered. "Come on, let's get back to the car."

Ryan's head whipped around. With an effort he kept his voice down. "Back? But—"

She reached out and took his hand again, and started to move back the way they'd come. He had little choice but to follow, or risk having the man with the rifle back outside, taking the dog's warning more seriously.

"We can't just leave," Ryan burst out when they were back at the road and the car.

"We're not. We're going to wait for Rand," she said as she pulled out her cell phone.

"But Trish could be—"

"I know, Ryan," she said patiently. "But do you really want to go up against a man with a rifle? And if he's got that, there could be more. And he wasn't the man in the picture, so he could be here also, and also armed. Not to mention the dog."

He couldn't argue with a single thing she said, but with every cell in him crying out to move and move now, listening to her reason was one of the most difficult things he'd ever done.

"Do you want to help Trish, or get yourself killed trying? Rand's the pro, and he's got the tools."

"Tools?"

She lifted a brow. "I'm assuming what he took out of his car before he loaned it to us were weapons of some kind. That was a pistol case, anyway."

He'd forgotten that, the small zippered case Rand had removed from the back of the SUV before he'd turned it over to them. And the metal box. Ammunition? he wondered.

He looked back into the woods while she made the call. He heard her update Rand on what they'd found. Heard her ask if she should call the local sheriff's office. She listened for a moment, then said, "All right," before ending the call.

"Cops?"

She shook her head. "He said not yet. Since a man with a rifle and a guard dog out here isn't that unusual, we'd need more to involve them. If we find evidence Trish is there—"

"Then let's go. We can at least watch."

"Somebody needs to wait up here for Rand. He said he'll be here in less than ten minutes."

"Then I'll go. Sasha, I have to do *something*."

He knew he sounded desperate, but then, he was.

"Wait." She reached through the driver's window and hit a button.

"Sasha—"

"No, I mean wait just a minute." She walked around to the back and opened the rear cargo doors. Ryan followed, wondering if she thought Rand had left a weapon of some kind. When he got there, she was already rummaging through the equipment locker that, given it had been open, Ryan guessed was empty of weapons after all.

"He's stocked up for everything here," she said. "Tools, first aid, water, so maybe…"

After a moment Sasha came out with a leather case that clearly held binoculars.

"Brilliant," he said, leaning in to take them. And that was his undoing, leaning in. She was so close, he could feel her warmth, smell the roses… He kissed her.

The jolt that went through him almost made him drop the binoculars. For an instant she stiffened, in shock he guessed, but then her mouth went soft, yielding. Heat singed along his nerves as the question he'd been carrying for so long was answered in fiery letters a foot high.

Yes. Yes, Sasha Tereschenko still sizzled his blood. She always had.

"Oh," she said when he finally broke the kiss, his pulse hammering. "That's…interesting to know."

He raised his brows in inquiry; actual words seemed beyond him at the moment.

"That it's still there."

"Oh, yeah," he managed. "It's still there."

He made himself concentrate on silently moving as he made his way back through the trees, her warnings and the promise she'd extracted from him to do nothing more than watch—and since he had the binoculars, from farther back—echoing in his mind. He'd keep that promise, he thought. As he'd told her, unless he saw Trish. If he spotted his little sister, all bets were off. And somewhat to his surprise, she'd accepted that.

"If it were my sister or brother, no one could stop me, either," she'd said.

As promised, he stopped short of where they'd been. Then worked his way to the right, where he'd have a better angle on that new building. It was the only clearly securable building on the property, and between that and the armed man, it had to be the place to watch. He lifted the binoculars to his eyes and zeroed in.

All seemed quiet. There was a window in the side of the building, but it had been masked off with what looked like a cut-up sign of some sort. But around the edges, here in the shadows of the tall trees, he could see light seeping through around the edges of the blockage.

Photography lights?

The idea hit him suddenly and nauseatingly. Could one of that man's twisted photo shoots be going on right now? Was the reason Trish wasn't up on his sick Web site because the pictures hadn't been taken yet? Were they being taken right now, while he sat up here like a frightened rabbit?

The promise he'd made Sasha tugged at him. His common sense told him the fact that lights were on in that building wasn't evidence that Trish was there. But his gut was screaming, and he didn't think he could rein it in much longer.

You're just a tech-head, he told himself. *What the hell can you do? This isn't a game. We're talking real guns here.*

He'd never felt more useless in real life. Maybe Sasha was right, had been right all along. He'd lived too much in the virtual world, and not enough in the real one. He'd—

"Anything?"

He nearly yelped as Rand's voice came from almost directly behind him. Rand was a big guy, and he hadn't heard a thing.

"No. Except there are lights on."

He turned as he gestured toward the window. Only then did he notice the green camouflage jacket Rand had on, and he suddenly realized how effective the dappled clothing was.

There was a leather case, about twice the size of the binoculars case, around his neck.

"Give me a few minutes," Rand said. He pulled a green knit cap out of a pocket and put it on, apparently to mask the gleam of his pale hair. To Ryan's surprise he unrolled the brim down over his face, and it became clear it was a ski mask that made him seem to blend into the greenery even more.

"There's a dog," Ryan warned.

Rand nodded; Sasha must have told him. Sasha, who was hopefully waiting safely up by the car, Ryan thought as Rand moved away with a silence that seemed impossible. He didn't want to have to worry about two of the women he loved—

Damn.

Had he really thought that? After barely two days back in her company, was he in even deeper than before? He'd spent more hours with her in their short time together than any woman he'd ever dated. He'd liked her then, more than he'd ever liked a woman. Wanted her even more than that. Whether that added up to love was something he hadn't had time to figure out before she'd made her decision and walked out.

He didn't blame her, now. Looking back, he could see her reasons, from her point of view, were good ones. He had been too young, too carefree. Too focused on having fun, taking little seriously. And most of all, she'd been right that he took his family for granted. Nothing had taught him that more soundly than the past week.

So where did that leave them now? Would she give him another chance? She'd kissed him back. Oh, yeah, she'd kissed him back all right. She—

Again he nearly yelped when the undergrowth barely three feet away moved and Rand rose up before him. With a quick shake of his head, he gestured back up toward the road. Moments later they were back at the car, Rand was shrugging off the jacket he didn't really need on this warm day, and Sasha, amazingly, came over and took Ryan's hand once more.

"Sorry, Ryan," Rand said. "It's not the place."

"But the gun, the dog," he began, stopping when Sasha's fingers tightened around his. The contact helped him focus, calm down a little.

"Oh, there's reason for them," Rand said. "But it's not porn."

"How could you tell, from outside?" Sasha asked.

Rand opened the leather case he'd just taken from around his neck. He took out an odd-looking piece of equipment that looked sort of like the binoculars but bigger, with a single, flat-screened viewer instead of two eyepiece lenses, dials and an odd array of other controls attached.

"One of Ian's newest babies," Rand said.

"Infra-red?" Sasha asked.

"No," Ryan answered, recognizing the piece. "It's based on millimeter wave technology. Like the newer stuff they use at airports."

Sasha's brows rose. "You mean the stuff that can see through your clothes?"

"More important," Rand said, "through the sign they were using to mask the window. Ian's got it fine-tuned and en-hanced enough it can even see through some walls. It's a great tool."

"As long as you're the good guys," Sasha said, sounding a tiny bit wary.

"Good thing we are, then, isn't it?" Rand said with a smile as he put the device back into the locker.

"What did you see?" Ryan asked; he'd already accepted Rand's assessment that this wasn't the place. Such was the rep-utation of Redstone Security.

"They've got a major pot farm going in there."

It seemed anti-climactic after all the tension and evil imaginings.

"Now what?" Ryan asked dispiritedly.

"We keep going," Sasha said firmly.

"Yes," Rand agreed. "I talked to Kate as soon as she got out of her meeting. She has a friend who works at the college, in the offices. She called her, and I'm going to meet with her, ask about the possibles." He glanced at his watch. "I'm going to have to hustle to make the agreed time."

"What about that?" Sasha asked, nodding toward the driveway that led to a hemp smoker's dream. "Are you going to tell the police?"

"Later. They're not going anywhere, and Trish comes first."

And that, Ryan thought, was why he loved Redstone.

Sasha knew Ryan was disheartened. She, too, had thought they'd found what they'd been looking for. As they got back in the car after Rand had left for his meeting at the school, she pondered what to do next.

"Shall we follow him to the school?" she asked.

Ryan shrugged. "Why duplicate? There must be something else we can do."

"This afternoon we can go back to the café, talk to some of the kids who maybe might remember this sleaze," she said.

"And in the meantime?" he asked as he started the car and turned to head back to the highway.

"I'm thinking," she said.

And she was. This case was more difficult because Trish wasn't a child, where people instinctively paid more attention to anything unusual. It was more difficult because she'd come here apparently voluntarily, so she wouldn't have stood out or likely made a fuss until it was too late.

"Let's go back by the other house," she finally said. She wasn't sure why, exactly, just that it had stuck in her mind and been niggling at her even as they'd thought they'd struck gold.

"The landscaper's paradise?"

"Yes." Interesting, she thought, that he assumed that was the one she'd meant. But the guy with the broken leg eliminated the other one. Unless, of course, he was faking it. Or had a partner, an accomplice.

Don't overly complicate it, she told herself. *Time enough for that later if things start to look that way.*

Ryan drove silently, and Sasha noticed he wasn't checking

the GPS for directions, but doing it from memory. She was a bit amazed; what they'd thought they'd found would have blasted all this out of her mind if it had been her own sibling in trouble.

But then, Ryan Barton had an exceptional brain. She'd always known that.

He also had an exceptional mouth. Among other things.

Heat flushed her face, and she turned her head to look out the passenger window, not wanting him to see. He'd become too perceptive. He'd probably guess the source of her blush.

By the time the car slowed as they neared the expansive, perfectly maintained yard, she was back in control.

For a moment she simply sat, looking at the geometric pattern, the mirroring of one side to the other, the absence of even the slightest weed or bit of moss in a place where fighting them was a constant battle. Nothing had changed. There was still no sign of the car that had led them to this address, and no sign of anyone at home.

"It's too perfect," she murmured as she stared.

"Too much work," Ryan said. "I hope they pay somebody to do it."

"And if they do, can you imagine the instructions?"

"Probably start with the words *immaculate* and *scrub brush* and go downhill from there."

Sasha gave him a smile as she nodded in agreement with his quip. He was doing well, she thought, handling the disappointment of not finding Trish at the guarded compound in a way she wasn't certain he'd have been capable of two years ago.

Or perhaps she'd simply underestimated him, assumed that the surface charm and lightheartedness was all there was, and had never truly looked at the foundation it was built on.

"So what kind of person demands such perfection?" she asked.

Ryan's brow furrowed. "A control freak?" he suggested.

She glanced at him. "Maybe. Or…someone who needs control here because he's out of control somewhere else?"

Ryan went very still. "I hadn't thought of that. That the perfect garden might be…a sign."

"Of an imperfect mind?" She looked back at the garden. "Perhaps a public display for someone with traits not so suited for public display?"

"Or maybe someone who doesn't have those traits himself, but is living with someone who does?"

Sasha turned sharply. "And reacting to that? Oh, now there's a thought."

Ryan looked pleased at her words, as if they'd warmed him somehow. The idea that she had the power to do that warmed her in turn. When this was over, when Trish was safe…well, they'd just have to see.

"Merits a closer look, given all that," Sasha said, and opened the car door.

Ryan was right beside her. They walked around the house, peering in the windows, most of them masked with lacy curtains that made Sasha think of her mother's love of things Victorian. From what they could see, the interior matched the exterior, immaculate, with not a book or magazine visible, let alone out of place. The furniture gleamed like polished metal, even in the dim light of the closed-up house.

"There could be an inside room, without windows, that we can't see," Sasha said as they completed the circuit.

"I don't think so," Ryan said. "Judging from the rooms we could see, the only windowless room is that one bathroom we could see into through the kitchen. Given the footprint of the house, and the size of the rooms, I don't think there's any un-accounted-for space."

Bless that computerlike brain, Sasha thought.

"Unless there's a basement," she said. Ryan winced. She didn't blame him; it was such a horror-film cliché. "But as damp as it is up here, I'm not sure they do full basements much."

"And there's no outside access."

She didn't mention that for the kind of purposes they were talking about, outside access would be a detriment.

"I want a closer look at the greenhouse," she said.

The building was solid wood at one end, with an extended greenhouse of Plexiglas panels nearly fifteen feet long. It wasn't locked, and they stepped inside. It was as carefully kept as the rest of the premises, even the gravel beneath the potting bench at one end scrupulously clean of spilled soil.

"Nuts," Ryan muttered as they walked between the carefully tended plants in various stages of growth.

"I'm betting the moment a plant starts looking tired, out it goes, to be replaced by an understudy," Sasha said, waving at the length of the plant tables.

The shed end of the building was in the same immaculate order. And there was no place to hide anything. They walked toward the last building on the property, the garage. There was a small side-entry door that she tried, a little surprised that it opened. Sasha looked around at the empty space, the tidy cabinets and a floor so clean you'd never know you were in a garage.

"Perfect as the rest," Ryan said. "But…"

"Something?" she asked after a moment.

He shook his head, then stepped into the garage. He looked around, although there was nothing Sasha could see to really look at. But when he came back to the door, she saw an expression on his face that told her to be quiet until he worked out whatever he was thinking. He stepped outside and walked to one side of the garage, then backed up a few feet and simply looked.

Sasha closed the small door and followed.

"Ryan?" she finally asked, unable to wait any longer.

"It's too long," he said.

"What?"

"It's at least eight feet longer on the outside than the inside space."

Sasha's pulse picked up. She didn't ask if he was sure. She knew he was.

They hurried toward the back of the garage.

"There," Ryan said, pointing at the side wall. Sasha looked, saw a faint change in paint color, fresher against faded, as if one section had been painted more recently.

There was no sign of a door or any other kind of entry, only a lean-to, three-sided structure against the back wall, the kind put up for storage of garden tools. They walked toward it.

Ryan stopped dead two feet away. When he spoke, it was nearly a whisper. "It's locked."

She saw the shiny hasp and padlock on the door. And instantly got why he'd sounded like that. "And nothing else was. Not the greenhouse, the shed or even the garage."

He nodded.

"Let's check Rand's toolbox in the back. Maybe there's something we can pry it open with."

If the illegality of that even occurred to Ryan, he ignored it. "Never mind that," he said. "Just find me something I can use as a screwdriver. I've got a Swiss Army knife on my own key chain, but it's back at Rand's place."

"Hang on," Sasha said, smothering a grin she was afraid was inappropriate at this moment. She ran out to the car and grabbed her brightly colored felted bag, digging into the bottom as she ran back. As she arrived back at where Ryan was tapping on the sides of the lean-to, she was pulling out her own key chain. With her own little red knife hanging helpfully next to her car key.

Ryan looked at it, then at her. In that moment something passed between them, something that was acknowledgment and promise, something that made her pulse kick up yet again.

He went to work, and Sasha quickly saw what he was going to do.

"A hasp like this is only as good as what it's fastened to," he said as he got the first screw holding it to the wooden door going. The little knife did a quick job, and within a couple of minutes, the shiny padlock was still holding, but the hasp was no longer fastened to the door. It swung open freely.

For a moment, Sasha thought it had all been for nothing.

There was an assortment of typical garden tools lined up neatly in a rack on the garage wall, and apparently nothing else in the shed.

"A second set?" Sasha said, recalling the similar tools they'd seen in the greenhouse shed.

"These have never been used," Ryan said. She looked closer, saw he was right; these bore no scratches or marks or any sign of ever having touched dirt. "And why lock these up, but not those?"

She heard Ryan's breath catch.

"Camouflage," he said, and began to move the tools away from the back wall. Sasha wasn't sure what he meant, but helped him set them aside. And then she saw it.

"Ryan!"

She pointed downward. About three feet from the ground. He leaned forward, saw what she had seen. A hinged door. Almost like a doggie door, only larger. Larger enough for a person.

Even a stocky, beefy-shouldered man.

Ryan was on his knees in an instant, pulling at the door. The man had apparently counted on the outer lock, for this was only latched. In seconds Ryan had it open and was scrambling through.

"Trish?"

She heard him yell it, so knew before she got inside after him that his sister wasn't immediately in sight. But the paraphernalia of the Web site was.

Lights, camera, action, she thought grimly as she looked around. And at one end of the room was the computer setup, from where he likely ran his little enterprise, and lured unsuspecting girls into his web.

"Damn it!" Ryan's frustration echoed off the walls of the apparently unoccupied room. "Where is she? What did he do with her? And where is he, did he run, is he—"

"Hush!" Sasha said, holding up a hand. Ryan stopped his tirade midstream.

And there it was again, a faint thud and a barely perceptible rattle.

"Again, so we can find you!" Sasha yelled to the room.

There was no voice, but the thud came again, twice. Louder this time, leading them to the back corner. Hidden from the rest of the room by a stub wall was a small closet, maybe four by four, with a door secured by a dead bolt on the outside.

Ryan got to it before she did. He twisted the knob and yanked the door open.

The girl was lying naked on the floor, her arms and ankles bound together with duct tape. The silver stuff was also over her eyes and mouth. She was obviously terrified, and had clearly been crying. She was bruised in several places and bleeding from more than one scrape.

But she wasn't dead.

And she wasn't Trish.

Sasha sat in the backseat with Courtney—the girl had told them her name after Sasha had painstakingly peeled the duct tape from her mouth, trying to cause the least pain possible— rocking her gently, simply repeating, "It's over, you're safe," knowing it would take time for the girl to accept. She had her arm around quivering shoulders wrapped in the first-aid blanket from Rand's well-stocked locker.

She had found the locker also contained some latex gloves, and had donned them in an effort to preserve any evidence that might be on the tape. She'd sensed the change in Ryan at that moment; he knew enough to realize why she was doing it, and the tacit acknowledgment that this was a crime scene. She guessed he also knew this was no longer going to be a private investigation, and no longer only about Trish. She knew she didn't need to explain the up and down sides of that. It was enough that he had to deal with the disappointment of not finding his sister.

"I'm calling Rand," Ryan said. "If I know Redstone, he's got some juice with the sheriff, and it would be better if he made the call."

Sasha nodded, and he walked away a few feet with cell phone

in hand. This was going to be complicated. Since Trish had been lured across state lines, they could even end up with the feds involved, although she knew the laws in the area of adult Internet luring were a bit murky, and different from state to state.

She appreciated that Ryan seemed to realize he should keep his distance from the traumatized girl. Courtney had barely managed to tell them her name.

But now she seemed, if not calmer, at least more inclined to talk, and Sasha knew they had limited time before the authorities arrived and took it all out of their hands. Using every bit of her training and knack for empathy, she encouraged Courtney to talk. And although she was difficult to understand through her weeping, Sasha was able to figure out that she, like Trish, had just turned eighteen, and she'd been in the clutches of their Internet predator only since yesterday. Not that the girl knew it—she said she'd been locked up in that closet with the tape over her eyes when not actually forced to pose for his lewd photos—and had no idea how much time had really passed.

Ryan came back, done with the call to Rand. "He's on it. Making the call and on his way here."

"The police?" Courtney asked, making a visible effort finally to control her sobbing.

"They'll be here. And they'll notify your family."

"Oh, God—" a hiccup interrupted her as she choked back another wail "—my mom's gonna freak."

"Your mother will just be glad you're safe," Sasha assured her.

"I was so scared."

"Of course you were. It was horrible."

"I thought he was real. Gentle, sensitive. He was like a poet, you know?" A fresh wail broke from her.

"He was very, very good at this, Courtney. You weren't the only one who bought it."

"I know." She shivered violently. "That's why I was so scared. I knew he'd had another girl here, before me."

Even though he was a couple of feet away, Sasha sensed

Ryan go rigid. *Don't talk,* she urged him silently, afraid it would destroy the fragile effort Courtney was making to stay in control.

"How did you know that, Courtney?"

"He told me. That's why I had to do what he said." She gulped in a deep breath.

"Courtney?" Sasha prodded, very gently, after a moment.

"He said he'd kill me if I didn't."

Another deep breath before she added the words Sasha had feared.

"Just like he killed her."